Get Your *Coventry Romances* Home Subscription NOW

And Get These 4 Best-Selling Novels *FREE:*

LACEY
by Claudette Williams

THE ROMANTIC WIDOW
by Mollie Chappell

HELENE
by Leonora Blythe

THE HEARTBREAK TRIANGLE
by Nora Hampton

A Home Subscription! It's the easiest and most convenient way to get every one of the exciting Coventry Romance Novels! ...And you get 4 of them FREE!

You pay nothing extra for this convenience: there are no additional charges...you don't even pay for postage! Fill out and send us the handy coupon now, and we'll send you 4 exciting Coventry Romance novels absolutely FREE!

SEND NO MONEY, GET THESE

FOUR BOOKS FREE!

C0981

MAIL THIS COUPON TODAY TO:
COVENTRY HOME SUBSCRIPTION SERVICE
6 COMMERCIAL STREET
HICKSVILLE, NEW YORK 11801

YES, please start a Coventry Romance Home Subscription in my name, and send me FREE and without obligation to buy, my 4 Coventry Romances. If you do not hear from me after I have examined my 4 FREE books, please send me the 6 new Coventry Romances each month as soon as they come off the presses. I understand that I will be billed only $9.00 for all 6 books. There are no shipping and handling nor any other hidden charges. There is no minimum number of monthly purchases that I have to make. In fact, I can cancel my subscription at any time. The first 4 FREE books are mine to keep as a gift, even if I do not buy any additional books.

For added convenience, your monthly subscription may be charged automatically to your credit card.

☐ Master Charge **42101** ☐ Visa **42101**

Credit Card # ____________________

Expiration Date ____________________

Name ____________________
(Please Print)

Address ____________________

City ____________ State ____________ Zip ____________

Signature ____________________

☐ Bill Me Direct Each Month **40105**

Publisher reserves the right to substitute alternate FREE books. Sales tax collected where required by law. Offer valid for new members only.
Allow 3-4 weeks for delivery. Prices subject to change without notice

Simon's Waif

by

Mira Stables

FAWCETT COVENTRY • NEW YORK

SIMON'S WAIF

This book contains the complete text of the original hardcover edition.

Published by Fawcett Coventry Books, a unit of CBS Publications, the Consumer Publishing Division of CBS Inc., by arrangement with Robert Hale Limited

Copyright © 1980 by Mira Stables

All Rights Reserved

ISBN: 0-449-50207-4

Printed in the United States of America

First Fawcett Coventry printing: September 1981

10 9 8 7 6 5 4 3 2 1

Simon's Waif

One

He had hoped for a couple of hours on the river with his rod, but the day was too bright. The fish would not be stirring. And by the time the evening rise began it would be dinner time, and Mrs Bedford would be distressed if he allowed her carefully planned meal to spoil.

Alert to her master's every movement, Meg got up from her place in front of the bookroom fire and came to rest a supplicating head on his knee. The pen flung down indicated that he was weary of his endless preoccupation with matters beyond her ken. Now was the moment to persuade him out of doors. She lifted melting brown eyes to his and crooned softly in her throat.

Simon Warhurst grinned. Meg disapproved of fishing expeditions. They were a shocking waste of time for a well-trained pointer bitch, but she would always accompany him out of doors, where countless tantalising odours set her nostrils a-quiver, even if she was not permitted to follow her natural bent. It was better than lying at ease in the comfortable book-room.

"Your turn this time, old girl," he told her cheerfully. "Too sunny for fishing, but just the thing for a gentle stroll, which you, at least, will infinitely prefer," and he tousled the lean intelligent head with an affectionate hand.

When she was working, Meg was the most obedient game dog that Simon had ever owned. When on pleasure bent she had a will of her own, and was sometimes permitted to indulge this to the extent of deciding the route they should follow. Today she chose to take the winding path that edged the riverside woods. Once or twice she strayed into the woods themselves, to be sternly recalled, for that was a rough terrain, descending steeply to the river and treacherous with exposed tree roots, and Simon had no desire to break an ankle. Apart from these brief reminders of discipline they strolled along companionably enough, Meg usually ranging a few paces ahead, occasionally loitering to identify a particularly appealing scent. She was half a dozen yards ahead when she stiffened suddenly into characteristic pose, nose, spine and tail beautifully aligned, one forepaw half-raised.

Game afoot, thought Simon, more amused than excited, and came quietly up to the eager bitch to see what manner of game had so intrigued her.

From this point in the path a shallow gully ran down to the river, worn by a tiny spring, respectable in time of heavy rain but no more than a trickle in the August drought. It gave Simon a view clear down to the water's edge, and what he saw there brought a half-smile to his lips. For a respectable law-abiding land-owner, that was a reprehensible attitude, for the lads who were lying face down on the river-bank with their arms immersed in the water were undoubtedly poaching—poaching his fish, too. Shocking conduct. Only Simon, despite his thirty years and sober habits, had not wholly forgotten certain lawless escapades of his own youth. He even conceded that they had chosen the place well—save for the lack of concealment from above. Broken water on the edge of a deep pool. Just the place for a wily trout to be lurking in these conditions. But a sneaking sympathy and a degree of respect must not be permitted to interfere with the enforcement of law and order. He had no desire to apprehend the culprits, both of whom he had in any case recognised, but if they were not checked in their nefarious careers they might cross the path of some land-owner less tolerant than he, and find themselves in serious trouble. The penalties for poaching were severe. A boy's mischief could lead to a stiff jail sentence.

He had just decided that a sharp hail from above would probably be sufficient to startle them into running off, when the scene changed with unexpected rapidity. A small dog appeared, scrambling over the rocks that bordered the river, and making its way towards the intent poachers. A third lad, a stranger to him, came behind it. Thereafter, events happened so swiftly that there was no time to call a warning. The dog must have spotted the stolen catch lying in the shelter of the bank, for it suddenly emerged into plain view with a sizable fish in its jaws. Its depredations were fiercely resented by the original thieves, both of whom sprang to their feet and set off in pursuit. Simon saw one of them snatch up a heavy boot which they had been using as a fish trap and hurl it at the absconding pup. It caught the little creature on the side of the head and toppled it, fish and all, into the river. Possibly it was stunned, for it did not seem to be swimming. The strange lad, presumably the pup's owner, made no attempt to wreak vengeance on the aggressor. He stumbled down to the water's edge and dived in clumsily after his pet.

Suddenly the peaceful riverside was taut with incipient tragedy. The stream was deep and fast flowing, and it was immediately obvious that the newcomer was no swimmer. Forgetful of all caution, Simon hurled himself down the gully to the point where two frightened sinners actually welcomed his arrival, since neither of them knew what to do.

"Pull my boots off," he snapped as he reached them, and struggled out of his coat as they did so. A glance showed that the lad in the water had somehow managed to get hold of the pup, but it was also clear that his strength was about done. He was paddling feebly with one arm, losing headway rapidly as the current swept him into deeper water. A long shallow dive took Simon out into midstream where the river would carry him down to the boy. A few powerful strokes and he was able to grasp the light limp body before it submerged completely, but the tug of the stream was fierce, and it was as much as he could manage to get his inanimate burden to shore some fifty yards lower down. He was glad enough of the help of the two lads who had kept pace with him along the bank and now waded in waist deep to help him out. Their timely aid inclined him more kindly towards them.

"Get up to the house, Jem," he directed, as soon as he had caught his breath. "Tell Mrs Bedford there's been an accident, and to make a bedchamber ready, with a fire and hot bricks. You'd best get home, Peter, and out of those sopping breeches before your father sees you and starts making awkward enquiries. I'll see to the lad. Either of you know him?"

Both boys shook their heads. "Never seen him before, nor the pup neither, which is a queer-looking little beast and not one as you'd forget," volunteered Peter, with a jerk of his head towards the small furry body which was being diligenlty licked by a concerned Meg.

"And Meg's the one of us with the most sense," grunted Simon, turning his own charge face down on the turf and beginning to squeeze his rib cage with firm rhythmic movements. "Be off, the pair of you. I'll deal with you later."

His patient did not seem to have swallowed a great deal of water, but despite Simon's steady labours he showed no sign of returning consciousness. Simon began to grow a little anxious. The boy had not been in the water for very long, and there was no sign of any other injury such as a blow on the head to account for his state. An attempt to take his pulse at the wrist proved abortive. Either the pulse was too feeble to be detected or Simon's own exertions had rendered him too breathless to find it. Impatiently he wrenched open the boy's coat to feel for a heartbeat, and made a discovery. The boy was a girl.

It really made no difference, except that perhaps it accounted for her prolonged unconsciousness. Girls were sickly creatures and likely to be prostrated by circumstances that a hardy lad would take in his stride. Still, conceded Simon reluctantly, as he renewed his labours, the wench had shown courage, even if of a foolish, hot-headed kind, hurling herself into the river to the rescue of her pet, and she the feeblest of swimmers. He glanced across at Meg. She appeared to have been more successful than he. The pup was beginning to move under her ministering tongue, and to emit odd snorting noises, even though the movements were no more than involuntary twitches. His own patient remained inert, save for the slight rise and fall of her breast that showed her to be still breathing. There was no more to be done here, he decided. A warm bed and the services of a physician were called for. In the meanwhile, he briefly abandoned his disheartening task, cursed the kindly impulse that had caused him to dismiss young Peter, and stumbled a painful fifty yards upstream to retrieve his discarded coat and boots. The boots he pulled on thankfully and the coat he wrapped about the unfortunate child. As he did so a panting figure appeared beside him.

"Sir, I'm as sorry as I could be. I've changed me britches, and me father knows nothing of it, just like you said. I thought you might need some help, Sir. I'm not trying to sweeten you. I know I did wrong—and it was me that led Jem into it—and I'm not trying to escape being punished. I had to come back myself. I daren't send anybody else for fear of me father getting to know. But honest, Sir, we never dreamed of anything like this. Just a bit of an adventure, and me more to blame than Jem."

Despite his concern for the girl, Simon could not forbear a hidden grin. As he had reckoned, young Peter was good sound stuff. Since he was the only son of Simon's bailiff, this was satisfactory. Simon had recently suspected that the boy was kept too close to his books. In such circumstances the present outbreak was understandable. He would have a word with Pettiford, but such routine matters must give way to present urgency.

"Very good," he said equably. "You can help by carrying that wretched pup up to the house. No doubt its owner sets some store by it."

He did not know quite why he baulked at mentioning the fact that the owner was a girl. Obviously it would have to come out, but he had successfully steered clear of the female sex ever since his disillusionment over Fiona, and although one could scarcely count this miserable bit of flotsam as female—he reckoned she was little more than a child—still the idea was distasteful.

With Simon carrying the unconscious girl, thankful that her breathing seemed to be steadier and deeper, and Peter coping with a rapidly reviving pup, already wriggling against the restraint of his arms, the little procession made its way to Furzedown, Meg trotting anxiously alongside, to Peter's no small inconvenience, since her maternal instincts prompted her to leap up at him from time to time to assure herself that her protegée was still in good frame.

Mrs Bedford welcomed them as though the master was in the habit of bringing home half-drowned guests at frequent intervals. Peter was dismissed to the kitchen with instructions to ask one of the maids for a rough towel so that the pup should not sully her clean floor, and then to find it a box before the fire. Simon was directed to lay his burden on the day-bed, which had been covered with a blanket.

"If you'll strip off his wet clothes, I'll give him a good rub down before we put him into bed," she added, and Simon was obliged to explain that the seeming boy was a girl.

"Well I never," pronounced Mrs Bedford, quite unperturbed. "Then p'raps you'll send for Alice, Sir, and ask her to bring me one of the nightgowns out of the parish box, for anything of mine would go round her three times."

That was something of an exaggeration,

but certainly Mrs Bedford's comfortable figure was a striking testimonial to her own good cooking. She handed Simon his coat, adjuring him to be sure to give it to Featherby to be dried and pressed, and stooped to remove the girl's shoes and stockings. Simon decided that it was no place for him, but as he reached the door he heard Mrs Bedford say in a puzzled voice, "A stranger, young Jem said, but I'd swear I've seen that face before. Can't just put a name to it, but it'll come to me. Have you sent for the doctor, Sir?"

Simon said that he would attend to it, and made good his escape. Downstairs he found two very nervous culprits awaiting him. He was not really in the mood to deal adequately with their sins and doubted if the tongue lashing that he produced on the evils of poaching would have much effect. Certainly young Jem looked sullen rather than penitent. Simon rather thought that a good thrashing might have been more effective in his case, but since Peter claimed to have been the ringleader it was hardly appropriate. He added a sharp reminder that he would not be so lenient if he discovered further evidence of raids on his property, whether it be fish or game, and surmised from Peter's guilty expression that something of the sort had been in mind. That done, he sent Peter with a message to the doctor and went to change his wet clothes before dinner.

The doctor was an old friend, and having examined his patient and instructed Mrs Bedford as to her care was very willing to accept Simon's invitation to take pot-luck with him. Over the meal—which included fresh-caught trout, delivered at the kitchen door by two subdued boys as a thank offering for being let off so lightly—John Fearing expressed concern for the sick girl.

"Don't want to alarm you unduly," he grunted, carving himself a portion of roast goose, "but there's something amiss with that child. The ducking's nothing. That water wasn't cold enough to harm any one, and by your own account you had her out of it quick enough, but she looks to me as though she's been half-starved over a long time, and for one cause or another she's in a high fever. I don't want to bleed her. She could do with blood putting in rather than letting, if one could only devise a way of doing it. Certainly when the fever abates she will need a nourishing diet to build up her strength."

These heretical medical opinions were Greek to Simon. He listened respectfully and awaited further enlightenment.

"Best try and find out who she is," advised the doctor. "Otherwise you may find yourself responsible for her welfare for several weeks."

Simon shrugged. "It won't concern me greatly. Mrs Bedford will take charge. And there's nothing she likes better than someone to cosset and care for."

The doctor laughed. "I expect you're right," he agreed, "but be careful. Don't forget that if you save a person's life that person becomes your responsibility. And I suppose you might be said to have saved the wench's life. I doubt if Peter and Jem would have been so successful. It would serve you right, double-dyed misogynist that you are, to be saddled with a sickly girl child. Anyway she's in good hands with Mrs B. I left her fussing like a hen with one precious chick. I'll call in tomorrow and take another look at her—the girl I mean."

They went on to talk of other subjects, one of them the misdemeanours of Peter and Jem. Simon felt that he had summed up Peter's problem reasonably well, and John agreed, but Jem was a different proposition. The second son of a farmer—one of Simon's tenants—his sole ambition was to go to sea. He hated farm life, with what, to him, was its endless drudgery, and now it seemed as though his resentment was leading him into dangerous mischief. They discussed the possibility of persuading Farmer Coburn to allow the boy to follow his chosen career. It was not promising. Labour was valuable on a farm, and Jem was a sturdy lad. His father would not willingly part with him.

Next day found the invalid in sad case. She had recovered consciousness while the women were preparing her for bed, but had seemed too weak to talk, though able to help them in their ministrations by lifting her hands or her head as requested before dropping into an uneasy slumber. This morning, however, her fever had mounted to a point at which she was delirious, tossing and turning and moaning in her discomfort, refusing to swallow the nourishing broth with which Mrs Bedford plied her, though she drank cold water thirstily. The housekeeper admitted that she would be glad when the doctor put in his promised appearance.

This was not long delayed, and careful examination revealed the cause of the girl's malaise. "Why bless me!" exclaimed Doctor Fearing. "The child's got the measles. Well now at least we know where we are. But for all that she's a very sick girl, ma'am, and will need careful nursing. As I said to Mr Warhurst last night, it's my belief that she's half-starved and has little strength to fight a severe infection. A good deal will depend on her constitution. Have you discovered anything about her? Her name, or where she came from?"

Mrs Bedford shook her head but mentioned her notion that she had seen the girl somewhere before. "No doubt there'll be enquiries after her," she concluded comfortably. "Maybe she's run away from school and that's why she's so thin. They don't feed them properly in those places. Leastways Mr Simon always used to say so when he was a nipperkin. Though how she came by a suit of boy's clothes has me in a bit of a puzzle."

"And to cut off her hair she must have been pretty desperate," said the doctor thoughtfully. "Pretty hair, too."

Mrs Bedford agreed and stroked back the ragged wisps that clung to the girl's flushed forehead. They were a soft golden brown in colour and would probably gleam chestnut in sunlight, but they had been hacked short by a ruthless hand. Like the doctor she wondered what dire necessity had driven their owner to such mutilation.

"She'll feel better once the rash comes out properly," she said knowledgeably, and the doctor nodded.

"I'll take another look at her tomorrow. Meanwhile, don't tease her with solid food. Milk, if she will take it, or tea. And as much water or lemonade as she cares to drink."

Mrs Bedford escorted him to the door, expressing her gratitude for his support in dignified fashion. Then she returned to the bed, straightening the tumbled covers and tucking the girl's restless hands under the sheets with gentle fingers.

The heavy eyes opened. For a brief moment there was a rational gleam. "Auntie Bee," murmured the hoarse, weary voice, as the lids drooped once more and their owner drifted off into the realms of feverish nightmare.

"Harriet Pendeniston!" exclaimed Mrs Bedford. "After all these years. No wonder I thought I knew the face. But with her lovely hair cut off and so thin and miserable looking. What in the world could have happened to her? Thanks be to heaven that she found her way to me! The master must know of this. Little Harry!" And murmuring thus in agitated fashion she rang for Alice to sit with the patient while she went in search of her master to tell him of her discovery.

Two

Simon had ridden out on estate business and did not come back until it was time to change his dress for dinner, so Mrs Bedford had to wait until the meal was done before she could acquaint him with her new knowledge. In the intervals of tending the sick girl she spent a good deal of time in recalling her former acquaintance with Harriet Pendeniston, searching her memory for every detail that she could recall of the girl's unusual story. Her information stopped short some five years ago. Apart from that it was complete and detailed, so that when she sought an interview with her master as soon as he had finished his dinner, she was ready to pour out a full tale.

Simon was in a pleasantly relaxed mood, a satisfactory day's work behind him, an excellent dinner within. He bade the good soul to be seated and settled himself to listen, having first made polite enquiry as to the patient's progress. Still very feverish, said Mrs Bedford, but that was only to be expected. She went on to describe the one lucid interval that had given her the clue to the girl's identity.

"Old Pendeniston's granddaughter?" exclaimed Simon. "What in the world is *she* doing in such a state? I suppose I'd better let him know she's here. A damned nuisance. The less I have to do with that household, the better, but I suppose that even *he* has some natural feelings, and may be worried about the brat. It's only decent to put him out of his misery."

Mrs Bedford shook her head portentously and settled herself more comfortably in her chair. "As to that, Sir, you'll be better able to judge when you've heard the whole," she began.

Simon restrained a strong impulse to grin. Before she attained the dignity of being his housekeeper, Mrs Bedford had once been his nurse. He knew her narrative powers of old. It was fortunate that he had no work of particular importance to do tonight. Once launched she would be hard to stop, and although he was only mildly interested in her disclosures, he had not the heart to do it. A story concerning local characters would be better than meat and drink to her, and he owed her something for her willing acceptance of the waif that he had foisted on to her. He poured himself another glass of burgundy and prepared to show an intelligent interest.

"I'd take leave to doubt if the colonel knows anything of Miss Harriet's circumstances," continued Mrs Bedford, "let alone worrying about her. He never forgave his son for marrying her mother. Maybe if she'd been a boy he might have changed his attitude, 'specially seeing as how his present heir is no better than a madman and a wicked one at that. But that's nothing to do with Miss Harriet. I'd best begin at the beginning, Sir, else I'll likely muddle myself and you too."

When she accepted a glass of port wine to help her settle her thoughts, Simon realised that it was likely to be a long tale. He resigned himself.

"Miss Harriet's mother was Mary Johnson," she began presently. "You'll remember the Johnsons, Sir. Decent, self-respecting folk, and brought up their children proper, though it was little the son did to repay them for it. A nasty, mean-minded creature, Jonas Johnson, but Mary was a lovely girl. As bonny as a picture, and all the lads after her, for her ways were as handsome as her face. Only she'd have none of them. Should have been a boy, for all her winsome ways. All she wanted was adventure—travel. They say if you want anything badly enough you'll get it, don't they? Who'd have thought a girl born and bred on the Johnson's farm would travel half across the world? But so it was. There came a lady called Preston to stay at the farm. Brought her two children to seek the benefits of country air and fresh farm food. Born in India they'd been, her husband being a soldier in those outlandish parts, and frail, puny little scraps they were, but they thrived. My! How they thrived! And Mary all over them. What with listening to Mrs Preston's tales of the goings on in India, with tigers and elephants and rajahs and such, and what with the two little lads, which Mary always had a hand with young things, never one like her for rearing a cade lamb or a weakly foal, seemed as though she was under a magic spell. When Mrs Preston had to go back to India and begged Mary to go with her, there was no holding back. Maybe the Johnsons were reluctant, but Mary was all agog to go, and she was their darling."

She fell silent a moment, pondering the odd workings of fate. Simon's attempt to hasten the recital by offering to refill her glass met with a shocked refusal. "No, indeed, Sir. I never take more than one glass, and that only when I have been overset as I have today."

"I beg your pardon, but you were telling me about Miss Johnson and her adventures in India," reminded Simon gently.

"Yes. She seemed well suited with the life out there. Wrote regularly—I told you the Johnsons had brought her up nicely—had her taught to read and write, and weren't they glad of it? Happy as could be, she was. Then she met Henry Pendeniston. The colonel's son. I can see how it happened. Mary always had a tender heart for the weak, and that's what he was. Weak in health—which is why he'd been sent on a long sea voyage—and weak in character. Though maybe with such a sire, that's small wonder. It would take a strong man to stand up to the colonel. Whatever the reason, they met and married. Three years with the Prestons had taught Mary the ways of the polite world. She had always been a quiet-spoken girl and prettily behaved, but how her husband could ever have thought that she would be acceptable to his father is still a mystery to me. Maybe it was his fears on that head that wrought so powerfully upon his health that he did not live to reach England. Mary came home a widow, but with the promise of a child to console her. Which might have been expected to soften her father-in-law's heart, but did not. To be fair to him he did not cast her off entirely. There was money of her husband's, left to him by his mother. *That* she should have, but he would not receive her, nor take any interst in the child—Harriet. Mary was content enough. The money made her independent in a small way. She could bring up her daughter in comfort, if not in luxury, and send her to school when the time came. She need no longer drudge on the farm, and she had no further ambitions. The child fulfilled her needs. She doted on her, but she was not foolish. The little girl was brought up as *she* had been—taught the ways of household skills and management until she was of an age to be sent to school, and never allowed to think herself above her station."

It had been at this stage in the child's life that Mrs Bedford had become 'Auntie Bee', her friendship with the family entitling her to honorary relationship. Once Harriet had gone to school she rarely saw her, but she saw enough to realise that there was tension between Jonas and his sister, the man jealous of the inheritance that had brought comfort and independence to Mary, resentful of what he called her niminy-piminy ways, and venting his anger, when occasion offered, on his defenceless niece. The death of Farmer Johnson when Harriet was twelve did nothing to improve this situation, but life went on reasonably smoothly for three more years, when Mary Pendeniston died suddenly and left her daughter doubly orphaned.

Harriet left school and went home to the

farm. Fifteen was full young to leave school, opined Mrs Bedford. Whether the money was no longer available, or whether the girl was actually needed to support her aged and grieving grandmother, she naturally could not say, but she *did* feel that Jonas Johnson had had a voice in the decision and she wouldn't be at all surprised to discover that he had managed to get his hands on Harriet's money—for it should have come to her on her mother's death—and appropriated it to his own uses.

During Grandma Johnson's last illness, Mrs Bedford had visited the farm regularly, but she had been more concerned with her old friend's condition than with Harriet. Jonas was surly and unsympathetic as usual. She guessed that Harriet was hard-worked and probably got little thanks for all that she did. She was quiet, perhaps unnaturally subdued, but Mrs Bedford had set it down to anxiety for her grandma and in any case it was not her place to interfere. After Mrs Johnson's death she *had* called at the farm once or twice, feeling that she owed it to her old friend to keep a motherly eye on the girl. She had been surprised to learn that Harriet was going to London. Uncle Jonas had found her a post as under-governess to some smart London family. She had seemed to Mrs Bedford to be very willing—even looking forward to the prospect. It was not so very different, she had pointed out, from what Mama had done when she went out to India with the Prestons. Mrs Bedford had been dubious. A girl who had left school at fifteen was hardly sufficiently well educated to be a governess. And how had an ignorant oaf like Jonas Johnson heard of a post with a smart London family? She hoped the child was not being pushed into some menial post where she would be overworked and underpaid. And if her present state was anything to go by, that was precisely what had happened. At the time she had merely assured Harriet of her continuing affection and interest and extracted a promise that the girl would turn to her if ever she should find herself in need of help.

"And I'm thinking that's just what she's done, Sir. I believe she was making her way here when the accident happened. If she'd wanted to go to her grandfather, she'd not be using the river path. So it seems to me there's no need to be telling him that she's here. Not, at least, until she's back in her right senses and can say what she wants for herself."

It was a nice point. Simon had no wish to involve himself with Colonel Pendeniston, who was heartily disliked by the entire neighbourhood, and if the man had shown no interest in his infant grandchild there seemed to be no valid reason why he should do so. Mrs Bedford, of course, was prejudiced, partly by old friendship, more by the fear of having her protegée wrested from her, but from what he had heard of Pendeniston Place there was likely to be small comfort there for a sick girl who needed careful nursing. On the whole he was inclined to favour the suggestion that they should wait until the invalid was sufficiently recovered to express her own views. The interview ended on a very amicable note, Simon expressing the view that Miss Pendeniston could not be in better hands, Mrs Bedford accepting this as her rightful due but gratified that the master had seen fit to fall in with her view of the case.

The following day saw little change in the invalid's condition. She was, perhaps, a little less feverish, but still very restless and certainly not rational. However, she seemed to recognise Mrs Bedford, even through the daze of fever, for she swallowed her medicine and the various draughts and possets meekly enough at the good lady's behest. Simon, paying a punctilious visit to his uninvited guest, thought she looked a little better. He studied her with rather more interest now that he knew something about her, and told Mrs Bedford that he could detect no resemblance to the Pendenistons.

"And a fortunate circumstance *that* is," retorted the head nurse tartly. "No. She's the very moral of her mother in features and colouring, only slighter and more delicate in build."

Simon nodded. He did not make any comment, though he could not help remembering that Mrs Bedford had described the mother as very pretty. Little sign of beauty about this poor little rat! Still, it was hardly fair to judge her appearance when she was disfigured by the blotchy measles rash, and in any case no one should know better than he that appearances were not everything. He picked up one lax hand and felt for the pulse at the wrist.

The effect of this innocent gesture was startling. The girl flung herself away from him across the bed, wrenching her wrist from his hold and exclaiming in a hoarse whisper, "Don't touch me. Don't you dare touch me. I'll scream and scream and raise the house."

Simon sprang back rather as though his devoted Meg had bitten him when he stooped to fondle her. Even Mrs Bedford looked shocked and startled, though she was swift to beg the master to take no notice. The poor child was plainly out of her senses.

"Yes," agreed Simon grimly, "but one cannot help wondering what shocking experience she has undergone to put that note of terror in her voice. A feverish nightmare it may be, for certainly she has no cause to dread my touch, but somehow it struck a chord of memory that distresses and frightens her. That can do no good. I shall not visit her again until she is rational, and shall rely on you to report to me as to her progress and to acquaint me with her needs."

Mrs Bedford promised to do so faithfully, and Simon walked slowly down the long gallery to his own apartments. The hint of mental suffering had touched his sympathies more surely than the girl's obvious physical distress. For the first time he thought of her as a person, not just as some kind of pitiful waif who must be warmed and fed and could then be forgotten. For the days that remained before he was again able to speak with her, Harriet Pendeniston was never far from his thoughts.

Three

After giving her nurses cause for serious concern through four interminable days, Harriet finally drifted back to consciousness—and to a feeling of well-being and security to which she had long been a stranger. At first it was enough to savour the comfort of the soft feather pillow on which her cheek rested. It was so very different from the Cushing's attic which had been her pitiful refuge these past few years. The pillow there had smelled sour and felt as though it was stuffed with corks.

Memory of that pillow, of the straw mattress and the wretchedly thin blanket and coverlet that went with it, stirred other memories. Hideous, paralysing memories. She struggled up on to one elbow and stared frantically about her, seeking reassurance. She had fled. So much she remembered, but where was she now? And was she safe? The room was far different from any she had ever occupied or even seen. It was not smart, like the best bedroom at the Cushing's, but it was much bigger than her bedroom at the farm. There were three windows through which she could see trees, and there was a bright fire burning in the hearth. The furniture was old-fashioned but it was well polished, and her sheets and pillows smelled of lavender.

At this point in her search for some means of identifying her whereabouts, the bedroom door opened gently and Mrs Bedford came in carrying a tray. The anxious, wary expression on the sick girl's face vanished. She sat up in bed and held out both hands. "Auntie Bee!" she said joyfully.

Mrs Bedford set the tray down carefully on a small table drawn up to the hearth. "There now," she returned contentedly. "So you're in your right senses at last. And a fine dance you've led us all. Fancy taking the measles at your time of life! Old enough to have known better."

This affectionate but practical attitude had a very heartening effect on the invalid. "Is *that* what I've had?" she enquired with interest. "I must have caught it from the Cushing children. And I wish I *had* known better, because it felt perfectly horrid. Am I recovered now? Can I get up? And where am I?"

"A deal better than you've been these four days past, but you'll not set foot out of bed for another sennight at least, and then only if the doctor says so. As for where you are—why—you're at Furzedown. Mr Warhurst's place. I made sure you were coming here to me when he picked you out of the river."

"I remember jumping into the river," said Harriet, wrinkling her brow. "Mandy fell in. Where *is* Mandy? Is she all right?"

"All right? I wish you were as much all right as she is. The first day she was as good as gold. Scarcely stirred out of her box and never made a sound, but she's a taking little thing for all her comical looks, and the maids started making a fuss of her and giving her titbits. You never saw such a change in an animal. Reckons she's queen of my kitchen now, she does, and getting to be a right little madam. Climbs up into my chair and yips at me when I order her out. It's only impudence though. I must say she's obedient enough in the ordinary way. So no need to fret yourself about her. Now. Let me put another pillow behind you and then you must drink this broth before it goes cold."

Harriet drank obediently. For the first time the broth tasted good and she finished it all, to Mrs Bedford's satisfaction. There were a great many more things that she wanted to know, but her nurse said that she had talked quite enough. She must go to sleep again now.

"You'll soon begin to pick up your strength if you just do as you're told. Then you can ask all the questions you want. For the moment it's enough to know that you're with friends, and that the pup you set such store by is thriving."

There was something very soothing about being treated as though one was still a child. Harriet, who, for the moment, had had more than enough of independence, snuggled down into her soft pillows and was asleep within minutes.

But this submissive attitude was born of weakness. Before the end of Mrs Bedford's threatened week she was clamouring to be allowed out of bed, even if only to sit in a chair by the fire, and was for ever pleading for a sight of her beloved Mandy. Mrs Bedford said that she didn't hold with dogs in bedrooms and thought that the convalescent might take cold sitting out of bed with no more than a borrowed shawl to wrap about her. The parish box nightgown had been exchanged for new ones of fine linen, but Mrs Bedford, having bought these, together with such essentials as a toothbrush and a brush and comb had called a halt. She had a strong notion that it would be easier to keep Harriet in bed if she had no clothes to wear. The boy's clothes in which she had arrived had been carefully dried and pressed, and Mrs Bedford, having hidden them away in one of her own capacious presses, felt that she deserved commendation for not enquiring into their provenance. Doctor Fearing had been very definite. On hearing of the girl's hysterical outburst he had strictly forbidden any enquiry into her immediate past until she was a good deal stronger. He was, however, more sympathetic than Mrs Bedford over his patient's desire to get up. He said it was a good sign, showing returning vitality, and added that surely, in a house this size, there must be something laid away in the attics or some such place that a bit of a girl could wear over her nightdress. To Mrs Bedford's objections that the said girl would never sit still in a chair but would be wandering about the room and looking out of the windows, he said only, "And a good thing too. What she needs now is something to distract her thoughts, and I don't want her spending too much time reading because her eyes are still weak."

"How about that pup of hers?" suggested Simon cheerfully, this conversation having taken place at the morning conference between the three of them. "At least that would give poor Meg some peace. The little wretch never leaves her alone, and now it seems to feel that it's a born hunting dog. Let the girl keep it with her. She can fondle it and teach it tricks. That won't strain her eyes. As for something to wear, I know just the thing. That quilted Chinese coat of Mama's. Pretty, and warm too. Can you lay your hand on it?"

Mrs Bedford thought she could, surprised but pleased that the master should think of lending his mother's exquisite coat to her young charge.

"And while we're on the subject of clothes, you'd better buy her one or two dresses and a warm mantle and some shoes. She will need to get out of doors as soon as she is strong enough, and she can hardly do that in a nightdress and a mandarin's coat, however glamorous."

As a result of these decisions Harriet found herself being helped into the most gorgeous garment that she had ever beheld. Of heavy saffron coloured silk, it was richly embroidered with a design of strange and fabulous beasts, interlaced with sprays of leaves and elaborate scrolls. The tiny upstanding collar would serve to keep the draughts from the back of her neck, said Mrs Bedford prosaically, and there was even a pair of soft yellow kid slippers to keep her feet warm, though these were rather too big. She immediately fulfilled all her mentor's dire prophecies by demanding to be allowed to look at herself in the long mirror, before being tenderly ensconced in the chair by the fire that had been carefully lined for her reception with a warm blanket. But one glance was sufficient.

"Oh dear!" she said despondently. "And the coat is so beautiful."

Mrs Bedford snorted. "A week ago you looked more like a ghost than a real live girl. There were times when I never thought we'd pull you through. Besides, that coat's not a colour to suit every one. You're too pale for it. Just wait till you put on a bit of flesh and get some colour in your cheeks."

"And if you would permit me, Miss, I could trim your hair. Make it a bit more evenlike," volunteered Alice, who had been helping with the proceedings.

Permission being willingly given—Harriet did not see how she could possibly look worse—Mrs Bedford at last succeeded in persuading her charge to seat herself in the chair, with a towel over her shoulders to protect the gorgeous coat, while Alice went off for her scissors.

She proved herself surprisingly adept, confessing that she often performed this service for the other maids and that she cherished ambitions of becoming, some day, dresser to a lady of fashion. Mrs Bedford huffed a little at that, but allowed that the result of her efforts was a considerable improvement. It was a pity that a short curly crop was not fashionable at the moment, but the hair would soon grow, and at least it no longer looked untidy and neglected. Alice withdrew, well pleased with this encomium, and Harriet, studying her reflection in the hand mirror, said, "I cut it off in the dark. I daren't make a light for fear of wakening somebody. That's why it was all ragged ends."

It was the first time that she had referred to the circumstances that had brought her to Furzedown. Mrs Bedford, obedient to orders, did not question her further, but produced a measuring tape.

"Mr Simon says I'm to buy you some clothes," she explained. "He wants you to get out into the grounds while this fine spell lasts, and you can't very well do that in your nightgown. Just a dress or two and a warm wrap," she added in conciliatory tones, reading all too well the mutinous expression on the pale little face. "It's no good protesting, child. You'd not bring disgrace on us all by being seen in those shocking garments you were wearing when you arrived."

Harriet said firmly, "But I have no money at all. I spent my last pence on buns in the village shop. I know I must have something to wear, but please, Auntie Bee, just one neat plain dress, the cheapest that you can buy. It may be weeks before I can find work and earn enough to pay Mr Warhurst back, and there can be nothing worse than running into debt when one can see no means of repaying it."

"Well I can think of one or two worse things," retorted Mrs Bedford sharply. She hesitated a minute. It seemed a shame to berate the little thing and she still so frail. But the stronger she grew the more difficult she would be to handle. Better to do it now. "Overweening pride is one worse fault. A deadly sin the Bible tells us. Just you try forgetting yourself for a minute or two, my lass, and think of other people. There's me that was at school with your granny, and friends all our lives. Knew *you* in your cradle. Are you too proud to take a kindness from me? Am I to drive you out to seek work—and you too weak to brush your own hair? And just remember that Mr Warhurst is my employer and that all my comfort depends on him. Am I to refuse to obey his orders—perfectly kindly, reasonable orders, too—just to satisfy your pride? Think of Mr Warhurst, too. Like it or not, you owe him your life. *And* the life of that mischievous imp of a pup. But for him you'd both have drowned. And now, when he treats you with ordinary Christian kindness, you'd throw it back in his face. Your Grandma would have been ashamed of you," she concluded, playing her trump card.

Harriet certainly looked suitably abashed but she was not wholly convinced. "Indeed I did not mean to seem ungrateful," she said placatingly. "You cannot know how much it means to me to be here and to feel safe in your care. That is a debt that no money could ever repay. And not for worlds would I make things difficult for you with Mr Warhurst. But I feel that it is quite improper for him to be buying clothes for me, and I am sure that Grandma would have said so too. So the least I can do is to accept a loan from him and determine to repay it as soon as possible. And surely you can understand that I must keep that debt within reasonable limits."

Mrs Bedford accepted partial defeat. The girl's attitude was so sensible and honest that she could not but respect it. What she needed, she decided, was an ally with wits quicker than hers.

"I think," she said slowly, "that it would be best if I acquainted Mr Warhurst with your sentiments on this head, and I hope you will be willing, then, to accept his judgement." After which she proceeded to take Harriet's measurements, scolding vigorously over her slight proportions and vowing that a newborn lamb had more meat on its skinny frame.

In view of this pronouncement Harriet meekly ate up all her lunch and made no audible objection to being obliged to rest on her bed for an hour after it. It was Alice who came to help her back to the chair, and she had brought a pretty blue ribbon that matched one of the embroidered colours in the Chinese coat. Between helping her into the coat, supporting her rather shaky progress from bed to chair, arranging the blue ribbon in her curls so that one or two could be coaxed to come forward over her ears and temples, and explaining that Mrs Bedford was dressing herself to embark on a shopping expedition on Miss's behalf, neither she nor Alice noticed the arrival of Mr Warhurst, a wriggling pup tucked under one arm, and Mrs Bedford, impressive in bonnet and mantle, at the door which the half-trained Alice had left ajar.

For a moment there was mild confusion, Mr Warhurst enquiring politely how the invalid did, Mrs Bedford making signals to Alice and reminding her in an under-voice that Miss Pendeniston should have her tea no later than four o'clock if she herself was not back to see to it. The confusion was brought to an abrupt conclusion by the escape of Mandy from Mr Warhurst's restrictive hold. The pup tore madly round the room, reminding Mrs Bedford and Alice of their differing errands, before hurling herself at her owner. A pug is not exactly a heavy dog, but the impact was sufficient to deprive Harriet momentarily of breath. When she recovered Mr Warhurst had picked up the pup and was lightly spanking her rump, adjuring her firmly to lie down. Her excitement being such that this seemed impossible, he sat down himself and gently forced the little creature into the desired position, keeping a controlling hand on her shoulders until she quieted.

Presently he looked across at Harriet, half-smiling at her rigidly erect pose as he said,

"If this young madam will allow us the privilege of five minutes rational conversation, there are one or two things that I would like to explain to you."

Her stiffness yielded a little at the description of the pup. She said in a shy little voice, "She is not usually so excitable. I expect she has missed me, although Mrs Bedford says they have been very good to her in the kitchen. Which reminds me to thank you, Sir, not only for pulling the pair of us out of the river, which Mrs Bedford tells me you did, but also for sheltering us both afterwards. I am most truly grateful."

"Well you could hardly expect me to leave you both lying on the river-bank, could you? That would have been shockingly untidy. Moreover, the opportunity of playing the hero at the cost of no more than a wetting had not previously come my way. I was disposed to make the most of it, and so was obliged to display my trophies to the admiring household in order to prove my tale. Though actually I can scarcely regard this wriggling object as *my* trophy. *You* really pulled her out of the water, and Meg did the rest."

It was the right approach. After the first disbelieving moment his nonsense banished the wary look with which she had been regarding him. Her lips quivered a little and he flattered himself that she had very nearly been betrayed into a giggle.

He said, a little more sensibly, "You won't have met Meg yet. She's a pointer—and, in my humble opinion, the best one ever, but lifesaving is no part of her normal duties. I think she must have been moved by maternal instinct. She had a litter of pups some months back. I should think this small wet helpless creature reminded her of their dependence."

He talked on, easily, pleasantly, telling her of Meg's care for the pup, of how the pointer had practically deserted him for two or three days until she was satisfied that the newcomer was familiar with the ways of the house and in a thriving way of going on.

You could practically feel the tension and the suspicion draining out of the poor little scrap, he thought kindly, and blessed the fortunate chance that had given him the key to a better relationship. He was not a conceited man; one ill-fated love affair had left him distrustful of his own attractions, but he had never before met the shuddering revulsion that this child had accorded him at her first partly conscious sight. It was comforting to verify that her attitude had been the product of some feverish nightmare. Nevertheless he felt that he must tread warily, lest he snap the first tenuous response to his overtures of friendship. He went on talking about the dogs.

Meg, he explained, had now returned to her allegiance. "Indeed," he added solemnly,

"I rather think that she now has doubts about the desirability of indiscriminate lifesaving. This wretched animal," he tousled the pup's ears, "gives her no peace. Poor Meg! She is three years old and accustomed to a quiet way of going on. Little Miss Pug is always ready for a game. Moreover nothing will convince her that she is not a hunting dog. At every opportunity she escapes the house and accompanies us on our expeditions, and whenever Meg points game for me—as she has been taught to do—Miss—Mandy, did you call her? bustles up and disturbs it, her whole attitude clearly exclaiming, 'Well—come on—what are you waiting for? Can't you see it's a nice juicy pheasant, only waiting to be taken'."

This time he won his rewarding chuckle, and it was pleasant to see the child's face light up with laughter.

He released the now sobered pup which trotted across to Harriet and climbed into her lap. She cuddled it close, regardless of her gorgeous trappings, and the wrinkled dark mast nuzzled her neck. Mr Warhurst felt that there was still a hint of desperation in the child's clutch on the silver-fawn body. It was soon explained.

He said carelessly, "How old is she? I'm afraid I know very little about the breed."

Her answer shook him out of his mood of satisfaction. "I don't know," said Miss Pendeniston. "About six months I think, but I can't be sure. I stole her, you see." And then, at his startled jerk of the head, "They treated her abominably and they were going to shoot her, so why shouldn't I take her? She loved me, and she was my only comfort. How could I leave her behind? I didn't take her collar. That would have been real stealing because it was set with brilliants. And I left some money for Horace's suit, so I'm not really a thief. But if you choose to hand me over to justice you may do so."

There was a sniff with this that sounded nearer to tears than defiance, but the stiffness was back in the pose, the cropped head held high.

Mr Warhurst said mildly, "Dear me! A dog thief! You're an enterprising little lass, aren't you? I begin to share Meg's doubts about indiscriminate lifesaving. Though if they were really going to shoot that lovable little creature, you did perfectly right to steal it. In fact, if I'd been on hand I'd have helped you do it."

The answer to that was a burst of tears. Mr Warhurst put one firm warm hand on the arm that clutched the pug pup, and said gently, "My dear girl. Don't you think it will be better if you tell me all about it?"

Four

The sordid little story was probably commonplace enough, reflected Simon. It was pitiful to him in that the girl was little more than a child, and that the two men who should have protected her innocence—her grandfather on the one side and her uncle on the other—had been wholly given over to self interest; and, though this was not quite so clear in his mind, because he felt that a gallant, eager young spirit had been battered and bruised almost out of existence. Not quite. He remembered with considerable satisfaction the 'theft' of the pug pup. Reprehensible it might be, if one were a strict moralist. Simon apparently was not. He hailed the act with thankfulness. No child who had been utterly broken would have ventured so far, and in defiance of the law, as she very well knew. And when he considered the scant equipment with which she had outfaced the death that threatened her pet, he found himself consumed with admiration. It would not do to show this, of course. Far better to accept the whole tale as though it was the stuff of everday living, and to concentrate on what was best to be done now. He found it difficult, however, to suppress his feelings about some of the characters who figured in the child's narrative.

The smart London family for a start. Mrs Cushing had social ambitions, but with limited means, a standing no higher than respectable and a husband who lived submissively under the cat's foot, she could only achieve her ambitions by stringent economy. The reception rooms and guest rooms in her Kensington house were tricked out in the latest kick of fashion. Her servants were underfed and underpaid. And since servants of worth and character would not put up with such conditions, she employed either inexperienced youngsters or those whose dispositions and abilities made them unacceptable in well run establishments. Dishonest, lazy, tale bearers and bullies, they made life even more miserable for the youngsters.

Harriet soon discovered that her uncle's tale of a post as under governess was sheer fabrication. To be sure she was expected to teach the children their lessons in the increasingly frequent intervals when successive governesses had given up in despair, but that was because she was the only one of the maids who could read and write. Fortunately Mrs Cushing discovered that she was also gifted with her needle, so she was eventually spared most of the menial drudgery that had been her lot during her first months in Kensington. She spent long hours cramped over her sewing, enduring the constant grumbling of a mistress who expected her to achieve elegant results with cheap materials, and straining her eyes by working in a bad light. Occasionally she was permitted the high treat of escorting the children on their daily walk. There were four of them, but the two older boys were at school and did not come much in her way, a circumstance for which she was heartily thankful, since they upset the two younger ones, who were quite bad enough as it was, always dissatisfied and whining and threatening to tell Mama if she ventured to correct them.

The advent of the pug puppy had brought a little brightness into this miserable existence, though it brought a new source of grief as well, since she was obliged to stand by and watch the little animal teased and tormented by her spoiled charges. At first she was able to restrain them with a reminder that Mama would be displeased if they hurt the puppy, since nominally it was hers. Pugs were fashionable, so Mr Cushing was instructed to buy one for his wife, who pictured herself driving in the park with her well-bred pet sitting beside her, resplendent in its smart jewelled collar, the envy of less fortunate females. Alas! Mr Cushing bought a puppy which was not even house-trained, far less carriage broke. Several betraying stains appeared on the drawing room carpet, and the puppy's brief reign as prime favourite came to an abrupt end when it tore the lace ruffles on Mrs Cushing's carriage dress. Harriet mended the lace and wept for the sinner, who had only been seeking to escape from the terrifying sound of rumbling wheels and did not understand why she had been beaten, and the pup was banished from the reception rooms.

Pugs are very intelligent. Within a month this specimen had learned to vanish whenever the children approached. She had a number of hiding places, but if hard pressed she would take cover under the hem of Harriet's skirt as the girl sat at her sewing, and Harriet had learned to lie valiantly to keep the little thing unmolested. She also managed to smuggle the pup up to her attic room at night, though this was for her own sake rather than for the pug's. The feel of the warm furry little body snuggling so trustfully in her arms brought her the only happiness she had known in that miserable garret. It did not take the little dog long to learn that the attic room was sanctuary. It took to spending much of its time there and Harriet came to look for its rapturous welcome when she climbed the stairs at night and would try to hoard some scraps from her scanty meals for its delectation.

So matters stood when Mrs Cushing acquired a new social asset. Admittedly she had to pay a higher wage than she had ever before paid to a manservant, but a butler who had once served in the household of the Duke of Byram would add such distinction to her entertainments as much make her the envy of all her acquaintance. The fact that Dorset (he had been born in the county, which entitled him, he felt, to lay claim to its name) had served his Grace in the lowly capacity of boot boy and in his own rightful name of Binks, and that the employment had terminated at the end of a month, to the vast relief of his Grace's butler, was mercifully hidden from his new employer, who set little store by written references. He was a tall, fine figure of a man was Dorset, and though he heartily despised the kind of establishment that the Cushings kept, it would suit him very nicely to lie low for a while, at least until the matter of the missing Murray silver had been forgotten. He did not think that anyone would look to find him in Kensington.

Unfortunately, in addition to a tendency to

light fingers and a certain vagueness about property rights, the fine figure of a man had a distinct weakness for women. His position of authority and his striking good looks made it a fairly simple matter for him to satisfy this very natural appetite. Such of the maid-servants as did not succumb to his masculine charms could easily be bullied into submission. It never occurred to him that the shy, quiet little sewing-maid or nursemaid or whatever she was might resent his distinguishing attentions. As a matter of fact she was not at all in his usual style. He preferred them plump and cuddlesome. But she had a kind of refinement that was mildly intriguing. Come down in the world, he shouldn't wonder. And then of all things, she turned out to be stand-offish. The sly nips and squeezes, the occasional stolen kiss that were the common currency of this kind of affair, were evaded with a skill that must be deliberate. Nothing could have inflamed him more surely. And one afternoon he caught her fairly, when there could be no evasion, following her into Mrs Cushing's dressing-room where she was hanging away a dress that she had been altering. He came silently up behind her and put his arms about her, nuzzling the back of her neck with greedy lips and squeezing her breasts with experienced fingers. He was quite unprepared for her reaction. She wrenched herself out of his careless hold with a strength that amazed him and swung round on him in a fury, her hands coming up almost automatically to slap his face, first on one side and then the other.

"Keep your hands to yourself in future, you dirty beast," she said, low and fierce. And turned and left the room before he had done fingering his burning cheeks.

Of course he could not leave it at that. He would take her now, whether his heart was in it or not. No uppity wench was going to treat Jacky Binks—alias John Dorset—like that, and giggle over it with the other girls. The lady had a sharp lesson coming to her.

He went to her room that night. The door was standing wide open. In all the months of Harriet's occupation no one but herself and Jessy, the scullery maid who had the other attic, had ever climbed those stairs, save for the housekeeper on her occasional visit of inspection. Since the arrival of the pup, Harriet usually left the door open. The attic, which had baked all day under a July sun, was like an oven. The one small window did not open. And the pup, like all her breed, had difficulty in breathing.

Dorset had taken the precaution of ascertaining that the doors of the attics could not be locked, but he had never expected such good fortune as this. A shaft of moonlight falling through the tiny window showed him the sleeping girl, just as she had cast herself down on top of the bed, unable to endure so much as a sheet to cover her in the stifling heat. For so large a man he could move very quietly, an art in which he had had considerable practice. He stole forward, velvet-footed, flung himself on top of her, and seizing her in his arms clamped his mouth over hers as the simplest method of preventing any outcry.

Harriet, roused from the first deep sleep of utter weariness, was so dazed that the attack might well have succeeded. But he had reckoned without Mandy. The pup, also roused from blissful slumber, reacted far more swiftly than her human protector. She was not very big nor very old but her instincts were sound and she had a fine new set of teeth which she used to good effect on the marauder's legs. Two good slashing bites were quite sufficient to make Mr Binks-Dorset release his victim and howl his wrath to the receptive darkness. The pup broke into a series of menacing snarls and was obviously prepared to bite again, and Harriet's cries for help swelled the clamour which roused the whole house.

The outcome was a foregone conclusion. No one, from Jessy, always jealous anyway, who had run to waken the housekeeper, to Mrs Cushing herself who was finally summoned to pronounce judgement, believed Harriet's version of the events that had occurred. No one wished to believe them. Mrs Farson, the housekeeper, herself had an eye to the handsome Dorset. So far as Mrs Cushing was concerned, an abigail, even one who was handy with her needle, was more easily replaced that her latest acquisition. Dorset stuck to his story that he had heard the girl cry out—perhaps in her sleep, he added with a large generosity—and had immediately gone to search for possible intruders, when he had been set upon by the dog and savagely bitten. No one enquired what he had been doing on the attic stairs in the first place, or how he imagined that an intruder could have gained access to the attics. Mrs Cushing said that a doctor should be summoned immediately to dress his wounds and promised that the savage brute which had inflicted them should be destroyed first thing in the morning. Dorset declined the services of the doctor, saying bravely that he could manage well enough for himself, but adding in a sanctimonious voice that he could not see his way to working in the same house as one who had so maligned him and that, with deep regret, he must tender his resignation. Mrs Cushing, who had feared something of the sort, promptly assured him that there was no need for such extreme measures. The girl should be sent off at once, and without a character, too. One could not give a reference to a proven liar. Which caused Dorset to smirk his satisfaction and Harriet to lose her temper and declare hotly that she would rather leave without a character than share the same roof with a dirty lecherous beast. She was promptly told to hold her wicked tongue and bustled back into her room by the scandalised Mrs Farson. Mandy had already taken refuge under her bed and came creeping out to greet her, not sure whether she was to be scolded or praised for her recent activities.

Harriet gathered the shivering pup in her arms and found relief in a hearty burst of tears which trickled down on the pup's fur and caused it to lick her face in a frantic attempt at comfort.

Presently the storm of tears subsided and she brought herself to face the problem of the future. One thing was certain. She was not going to let them kill the puppy. So she must leave the house that night and take Mandy with her. And there was one piece of good luck. Her pitiful wages had been paid only the previous week, so she had a small store of money. She had nowhere to go except the farm. Since coming to Kensington she had never heard from Uncle Jonas, but he was not much of a hand with a pen. Now that she was older and could work harder he might find her more acceptable, though she dreaded to think what he would say about Mandy. She would face that battle when she came to it. Meanwhile the main thing was to escape. She lit her candle and began to dress.

She had nothing fit to wear to present a

respectable appearance on the coach, and the sight of a shabbily dressed girl carrying a pug puppy was likely to attract a most undesirable degree of attention. Not that she supposed any one would search for her, but she would not put it past Dorset to insist that sentence be duly carried out on the animal that had dared to bite him. Desperation sharpened her wits. There was a suit of Master Horace Cushing's hanging in the sewing-room awaiting her attentions. It would be rather large for her—he was a plump lad—but it would serve. And she could leave some money to pay for it so that they could not accuse her of stealing.

Breathlessly, with wildly beating heart, she crept down the stairs, barefooted as she was, and made her way to the sewing-room, not daring to make a light for fear of wakening any one. As she gathered the suit over her arm another thought struck her. Her hair. Well—this was no time for half-measures. She found the dressmaking shears and sawed through the thick plait into which her hair was confined at night.

Back in her own room she dressed awkwardly. She had no shirt and dared not venture into the laundry room in search of one. Her chemise would have to do and she could wind a scarf round her neck. It would look a little odd in high summer but it was the best she could think of. There was no packing to do. With strange pockets she would have all she could do to cope with her purse and the pup. She could not manage a bundle as well. In any case there was little that was worth troubling about except her Bible that Mama had given her. She could only wrap it up carefully in a piece of paper and hope that some day she might be able to claim it again. At least no one would venture to steal a Bible.

She left the pup's collar in a conspicuous place on the table in the hall and three of her precious guineas with it. There was no time for writing explanatory letters and in any case she had no materials available.

The journey to Holborn was the next difficulty. It was a long way—perhaps as much as five miles—and the coaches left early, she knew. Nor was she too sure of finding her way. Better to set out at once and put as much distance as possible between herself and that hated house before daylight. Her preparations had taken longer than she had thought and dawn came early at this time of the year. She shivered a little at the thought of venturing out alone into the deserted streets, but it had to be faced. And if there were any desperate villains on the prowl they would scarcely concern themselves with a lad and his dog. Later, in daylight, she would concoct some tale about being employed to take the dog to a new owner in the country.

In the event the journey proved memorable mainly for her growing hunger. She had been too wrought up to think of eating before they left Fetter Lane, though she had managed to book a seat on the Winchester coach without difficulty, having assured the agent that the pug was not ill-tempered, a character born out by the sight of an exhausted little animal asleep in her arms. She had lost her way several times between Kensington and Holborn, and eventually Mandy had needed to be carried for short periods. Surprisingly heavy she was, too, but her physique was not designed for prolonged exercise. It was questionable which of the pair was the more exhuasted by the time that they eventually boarded the stage.

She had reached Alresford some time during the early afternoon and had bought buns in a shop which she remembered from childhood. No one had recognised her. She and Mandy had shared the buns in the shelter of a hedge before walking on to the farm.

It had never occurred to her that she might find strangers in occupation. They were kindly enough and gave her a glass of milk, but they could tell her nothing of her uncle's present whereabouts. They had been living at the farm for close on three years. There had been some talk of Mr Johnson going to Canada, but they did not know if he had actually gone. Certainly they had not come across him at any of the local markets or hiring fairs, so it looked as if he had left the district. When they, in turn, began to ask questions, she had evaded their kindly curiosity, saying that she had friends in the district with whom she would beg a night's lodging.

A night in the woods, empty pockets, and a hunger that made her feel quite sick, combined to convince her that she must have help, and she had been on her way to seek out Mrs Bedford when the accident happened.

The long telling had tired her. She sat limp and drooping in her chair, her hands lying lax in her lap, the wan little face utterably weary. Simon was filled with a passion of pity which he had some difficulty in restraining. His instinct was to offer whatever kind of help the girl needed, but luckily Mrs Bedford had warned him of the stubborn attitude that she had displayed over the purchase of necessary clothing. He was still mulling over the best way of broaching this ticklish subject when Alice came in with the tea tray.

He was grateful for the interruption. The crumpled little creature in the chair certainly looked as though she would be all the better for a cup of tea, and Miss Mandy woke up and announced her readiness to take an interest in the proceedings. She was told, in a very firm voice to sit down.

"You must never feed her at table," said Simon. "If you do she will become a nuisance, always pestering for titbits, as well as getting too fat, which is dangerous with this type of dog."

He turned his attention to Alice's tray. He was not in the least hungry and never took tea in the middle of the afternoon, but it seemed to him that a shared meal might help him to establish better relations with his protegée. He despatched Alice to the kitchen for another cup. "And some of Mrs Bedford's cherry jam, and some bread to toast and a toasting fork," he added with a flash of inspiration. "I am very partial to cherry jam," he told her, as Alice bustled off. "Especially the way Mrs Bedford makes it. Do you remember it from your childhood?"

It was a far cry from the girl's miserable story to cherry jam, but it served admirably, with its reminder of homely, comfortable things that had once been familiar. And purely by chance he had hit upon a genuine link with Harriet's childhood, for Mrs Bedford had always been used to present her grandmama with a jar of the new season's preserve. She was still telling him how they used to have it for a special treat on Sundays, when Alice came back.

At Mr Warhurst's suggestion, Alice poured out. She also spread cherry jam on the bread that the master toasted, since it would not do for Miss Harriet to sticky her gorgeous coat. By the time the pair of them had finished with her Harriet felt about seven years old and wouldn't have been surprised if one or other of them had suggested washing her hands and face for her when tea was done. She also felt very much happier, as though in giving Mr Warhurst her confidence she had somehow rid herself of something foul and beastly. In fact, like the little girl whom at the moment she resembled, she felt clean and good again, but very tired. Perhaps tonight there would be no frightening dreams to make a mockery of sleep.

And here was Mr Warhurst calmly telling Alice to come back in half an hour and put her to bed. "For she has sat up quite long enough already but there are still one or two points that we have to decide."

Much restored by tea and toast and a little easy laughter, Harriet sat up straighter in her chair and tried to concentrate her thoughts. It was difficult, because the whole situation was dream-like. Who, for example, could have imagined either Mr or Mrs Cushing in Mr Warhurst's place? Perfectly at ease and pleasant in the company of a housemaid and a girl who had been dismissed without a character; handling the mischievous Mandy firmly but with kindness. It was all too good to be true and very soon she would have to wake up to real life again. But for the moment she was too sleepy to fight any more. She just hoped

Mr Warhurst wasn't going to make things too difficult for her.

Mr Warhurst had no such intention. "Be patient for a little while," he was saying gently. "I understand your desire for independence and I respect it, but at this moment you are in no case to earn your own living, and the only sensible thing to do is to submit to the care that will make you well and strong again. If you neglect your health now you may be sickly for months. Let Mrs Bedford look after you—which you must know will make her very happy—and accept the simple necessities that she is bringing you with a good grace. You *must* have two dresses you know. Suppose Mandy were to tear one of them—or you were to spill a glass of milk down it? And I may as well confess now that I told her to buy pretty ones. All the other members of the household have to look at you. They may as well have something pleasant to look at, while I can think of nothing more likely to prolong your convalescence than being obliged to wear dresses that were dowdy or ugly and ill-fitting. As for payment—you can eventually repay me in money if you so wish. I will undertake to keep a careful account of all expenditure, and since I am comfortably circumstanced there is no urgency. But you could repay me far better by helping Mrs Bedford. Once you are a little stronger there must be a dozen things that you could do to lighten her labours. She is not so young as she was, you know, and the services of a daughter—for I am sure she regards you in that light—could do much to make her life easier. What do you say?"

What could she say? His tact made it easy to accept his generosity. Perhaps, some day, she would repay him in money. Meanwhile, she said, "Thank you, Sir," with all her heart.

Five

For the next week she saw very little of her patron. He came each day with Dr Fearing to visit her, gazing politely out of the window, hands clasped behind his back, while the doctor enquired into her progress, turning to join with the doctor and Mrs Bedford in the discussion which followed. She lay meekly, the covers drawn up to her chin, while they debated what further activities might be permitted her. She looked the picture of docility, but day by day the tide of youth and health was rising within her, and the thoughts behind the childlike mask grew more and more rebellious. They spoke soberly of rest and nourishment and gentle exercise, and Harriet controlled a mounting desire to be up and about and exploring this new world to which chance had brought her.

She had craned as far as possible to view the house through her bedroom windows. At the far end of the frontage—the end opposite to hers—there was a fragment of a much older building, linked to the main structure by what looked like a long gallery. Enquiry had informed her that this was the last vestige of the original castle. Oh, yes, it had been a castle, though a very small one, destroyed by fire during the Civil War. The new house had not been built until the reign of Queen Anne, which was why it was so modern and comfortable. But the Warhursts had not cared to destroy the last remnants of the cradle of their line, and the present Mr Warhurst had taken a fancy to occupy the ancient apartments, a large room on the ground floor which he called his book-room—and aptly named it was—and the bedchamber above it. It was a pesky nuisance being obliged to carry every drop of water the length of the gallery, and the master was difficult, too, about the cleaning of the book-room, because there were so many papers strewn about, and if any one disarranged them he could never find what he wanted. Mrs Bedford herself had to supervise the girl who went in to clean up the hearth and to dust and polish the furniture. But there—nothing was really too much trouble if it pleased the master. Never a man like him, as all the tenants and villagers would swear, let alone his own household.

Harriet was quite prepared to share the general opinion. In fact, she went rather beyond it. To her, he was almost god-like. And small wonder, so kind and thoughful as he had shown himself. Perhaps the thing that had touched her most was the gift of a handsome collar for Mandy. It had arrived two days after their long talk, and when she had tried to thank him for it he had laughed, and countered her shy efforts by declaring roundly that a dog capable of dealing so adequately with an unpleasant customer like Dorset, deserved a real dog's collar rather than a flashy circlet of paste gems, and that it was really no concern of Harriet's being purely between him and Mandy. Mandy accepted her gift, a band of soft green leather, stitched with copper thread and studded with small copper medallions, with a lamentable lack of enthusiasm, since it set a curb on the absolute liberty that she had enjoyed since her emancipation from Town fears and restrictions.

With very different emotions did her owner delve into the boxes that held Mrs Bedford's selections for her wardrobe. There had been some small delay in the delivery of these, since the dresses had needed to be taken in to fit her slender figure.

"No more to you than to a sparrow," complained Mrs Bedford, "but we'll soon change that."

Harriet had no objections. With returning health she had regained her appetite and usually gratified the cook by returning well polished plates. Since Mrs Bedford further insisted on her sustaining nature with glasses of creamy milk or a 'drop of sherry wine and a sponge finger' to bridge the yawning gap between meals, it seemed probable that the good lady's prophecy would be fulfilled.

"But I told them to leave the extra breadths on all the seams so that we could let them out again if it became necessary. Which I hope it will be," she ended with a determined mien.

There were the two much debated dresses, one pink and one a soft green, and both very pretty as Mr Warhurst had promised. They were made in a lightweight merino cloth and the styles were simple as became a young girl.

"A bit warm for this time of year," commented Mrs Bedford, "but autumn's nearly on us and the evenings already growing chilly. No use buying you muslins, though I must confess I was sorely tempted by one or two of them. Such pretty materials as they make for you modern young things! But you'd have been needing something warmer before the month was out, and with the expense to consider it was out of the question."

There were shifts and petticoats and stockings and handkerchieves, but no more than were necessary to present a seemly appearance, and a pair of shoes with cut steel buckles that were sturdy enough for walking out of doors. To a girl who had long been starved of dainty clothing, the boxes held treasure beyond her wistful dreams. Her doubts allayed by the assurance that in one way or another she would be permitted to pay for them herself, she abandoned misgivings and yielded to a wholly feminine delight in trying on the dresses and shoes and fingering the softness of the underlinen. One further moment of doubt she had when for the first time she saw herself in the long glass dressed in her new finery.

"I look so different," she said hesitantly. "I scarcely know myself."

"I should hope you *do* look different," retorted Mrs Bedford smartly. "Your Grandma would never have held up her head again if she had seen you traipsing the countryside in boy's clothes. A regular hoyden you looked, and your hair all ragged ends. I do believe it's beginning to grow again," she added, surveying the short curly crop which, thanks to Alice's assiduous brushing was beginning to regain something of its natural lustre. "As for your appearance, you look neat and seemly, which is more important than you think. You'll be here some weeks yet, because it would be the height of folly to embark on a new situation before you had fully regained your strength. But a new situation will have to be found for you," continued the wily woman, who had been carefully prompted by her master. "Mr Warhurst lives very quietly and retired, but he has a large circle of friends both in Town and in the country. As soon as you are strong enough, he and I mean to put our heads together and I don't doubt but that we shall hit upon just the thing. A place where you will be well cared for and self-supporting. But appearance is very important in deciding these matters, however strongly you are recommended. It should not be so, but that is the way of the world."

A month ago, such a post as her good friend described would have represented the summit of Harriet's ambitions. It was surely odd that now, when she was favourably placed in the way of achieving it, it should sound more like a prison sentence, a closing of doors on all the resurgent life that was clamouring within her. She was in a fair way to becoming spoiled by soft living, she decided sternly; forgave herself on the score of convalescent weakness, and, being young, decided to enjoy the present and let the future take care of itself.

She wore the green dress, for no better reason than that it matched the green of Mandy's collar, though a disinterested observer might have told her that it set off her colouring to a nicety. Fully dressed for the first time in three weeks, feeling a little shaky and strange, she embarked upon a gentle stroll about the house under Mrs Bedford's guidance.

Disappointingly soon her legs began to tremble and she grew breathless. It was quite a relief when a maid came to say that the vicar's wife had called to see Mrs Bedford about the meeting of the sewing party—the charitably disposed ladies who made the garments for the furnishing of the parish box. She was thankful for the excuse to return to her room and lie down on her bed for a while, but she did not sleep. Her mind was awake and active, assimilating and sorting a jumble of impressions.

The house made no claim to grandeur. The rooms were spacious, furnished with an eye to comfort rather than to smartness. Only one of them, the one that her guide had called the Saloon, might be described as impressive, and then it was an impression of delicate beauty, appealing rather than commanding. Walls and ceiling were tinted ivory, but the doorways, the window reveals and the ceiling mouldings were decorated with a design of leaf and tendril picked out in gold and green, colours which were repeated in the French brocade curtains. Unfortuantely, the furniture was all swathed in holland covers, so Harriet was not able to appreciate the full glory of the room. Rarely used these days, sighed Mrs Bedford. Only when Mrs Pauncefoot came to stay. She was Mr Warhurst's sister, several years older than he. There had been another sister, Miss Dorothea, but she had died young. Mrs Pauncefoot did not come very often, being much occupied with the care of a growing family and a husband who was an important figure in government circles. Like Mr Warhurst she had been born at Furzedown and had a fondness for the place. Yes, Harriet was told, Mrs Pauncefoot was the master's only surviving sister, and the oldest of the family. He had one brother who came next. Viscount Warhurst *he* was, and he, too, was married. His wife was very beautiful. *They* never came to stay at Furzedown, although Lady Warhurst had practically grown up there, being a near neighbour. Nowadays, it seemed, she preferred the excitements of Town life. If one could believe all the tales one heard, she was by way of being a leader of fashion.

There was a note of disapproval in the housekeeper's voice when she spoke of Lady Fiona. Harriet could see no reason for this, save that after ten years of marriage there were no offspring of the union. And that, after all, might not be her ladyship's fault. She might even be deeply disappointed about it, especially as there was a title to be inherited. At any rate, she mused, Fiona was a pretty name for a lovely lady. Much prettier than Harriet!

It was difficult to think of *her* Mr Warhurst as being brother to a Viscount. There was nothing in the least high in his manner. She remembered how much he had appeared to enjoy that impromptu tea party. He had behaved like a perfectly ordinary man and a very likeable one. Perhaps he did not care for being 'toad-eaten' because of his noble connections. She thought how Mrs Cushing would have behaved in circumstances such as hers, wrinkled her nose in disgust as she pictured that lady's sycophantic gush and decided to forget all about Mr Warhurst's noble rank. Presently, she drifted into a light doze.

It was not so easy to forget, though. She woke to a doubtful state of mind, wondering if she should have treated him with greater respect, and did a Viscount's brother have some special title by which he should be addressed. Taking tea with Mrs Bedford in the housekeeper's room she laid this problem before her and was comforted to discover that she had not committed a solecism by addressing her rescuer as 'Sir'.

"He *is* the *H*onourable Mr Warhurst," explained Mrs Bedford, pronouncing the aspirate with care, "but for some reason they never use it except on letters. If you was to write to him you would have to address him so, but that's not very likely, is it? As for his consequence, there was never a man that cared for it less. That's because he's so accustomed to it that he takes it for granted, so he's pleasant and friendly with everyone. But, mind you, there's something about him that warns people not to take advantage. A proper gentleman is Mr Simon." With which she busied herself over the dispensing of tea, and began to tell Harriet about her conversation with the vicar's wife.

Once given the freedom of the establishment, Harriet's progress was rapid. There were so many interesting things to see and to do that she was never dull or lonely. With Mandy and occasionally Meg trotting at her heels she explored the grounds and re-visited the scene of her adventure in the river. On wet days she spent hours examining the many strange and beautiful objects that filled the cabinets in the Saloon and the other reception rooms. On one occasion Mrs Bedford asked if she would like to see the long gallery and the book-room. Mr Warhurst had gone into Winchester so they would not be interrupting him. To Harriet's diffident suggestion that perhaps he would not care to have a stranger intrude into his private apartments, Mrs Bedford returned a cheerfully casual negative. "Nothing secret about Mr Simon's affairs. It's just that he don't like his papers disturbing. To my way of thinking they're in such a muddle any way that he'll never make moss nor sand out of them, but he thinks he will. He's supposed to be writing a journal of his travels. Travelled a lot did Mr Simon. First the Grand Tour—which was commonplace among the nobility in his day—and then with his father in outlandish eastern parts. The late Viscount was quite famous for his knowledge of such distant places and their wonders. Even the ancient relics that had been dug up from hundreds of years before. He was always my favourite was Mr Simon, and no use denying it. I'd hoped he would have married and settled down to raising a family. But when Miss Fiona, that was his childhood sweetheart, upped and married his elder brother while he was away in foreign parts, he would have no more truck with women. Not that he wasn't always pleasant and polite when they came in his way, just that he didn't trust them any more. As for her—I suppose if she fancied the title one can't blame her, especially brought up the way she'd been. Poverty-pinched and always looking to the main chance, her family were. Daresay they talked her into it. Only we'd always reckoned she was Mr Simon's sweetheart so it was a bit of a shock when the betrothal was announced and Mr Simon away in Germany and knowing nothing of what was going on at home."

Harriet listened to the tale with absorbed interest. She had never met Viscount Warhurst but she could not imagine any girl preferring him to his brother. In her eyes Mr Warhurst was as near perfection as it was possible for a human to be. She was a little startled to discover that this god-like creature could be so shockingly untidy. Wherever you looked in the book-room there were piles of papers, some of them loosely tied together in bundles, most of them just separate sheets of all sizes. The room itself was surprising after the gentle comfort of the rest of the house. The walls were of bare stone, cut in huge blocks and, as the window embrasures showed, massively thick; and the hearth, swept and bare at this season of the year, would comfortably accept enormous tree-trunks. A thick crimson carpet and curtains of the same cheerful hue served to mellow the austerity of the stonework, and if only one could furnish the old leather chairs with gay cushions instead of piles of dusty papers, the room could be given a much more welcoming aspect. Harriet's housewifely instincts itched to set things right. She said, "I can see how difficult it is to clean the room when it is in such disorder, but here, at last, is a task that I can perform to help you. It is not heavy work to move each pile of papers separately, polish the chair—or table or chest or stool," she put in with a mischievous chuckle—"and replace the papers just as they were, so that Mr Warhurst would never know it had been done."

Mrs Bedford was inclined to demur at the idea of Harriet polishing furniture, but the offer certainly appealed to her tidy soul. It needed only for Harriet to say that while she heartily detested dusting she really quite enjoyed polishing, and the matter was settled, with the understanding that Harriet's ministrations would take place during Mr Warhurst's frequent absences. There was no time to study the papers that cluttered the room though the girl did notice that many of them were sketches of strange-looking birds and beasts and flowers while others were filled with a bold and forceful script. Later she was to realise that in spite of the seeming disorder the pages were all numbered and carefully annotated as to the place and the season of the year. Meanwhile, Mrs Bedford complained that the room struck chilly now that the sun was off the front of the house and they made their way back up the spiral stone staircase that gave on to the long gallery, where ranks of long dead Warhursts gazed serenly down at them, and then down the easy, shallow steps of the modern staircase at the other end.

Harriet was very happy. Only that morning Doctor Fearing had said that she might now spend a part of each day in sewing or reading, so long as she worked in a good light and rested her eyes frequently with a change of occupation. She would be able to help with mending the household linen and could feel that she was not wholly dependant on the charity of her host. And she would have the satisfaction of knowing that in her humble way she was serving the object of her adoration. If anyone had suggested to her that she was more than halfway to falling in love with Mr Warhurst, she would have been sadly dismayed, even shocked. One did not fall in love with a god. Mr Warhurst might be easy and pleasant in his ways but he moved in a world that was infinitely remote from the world of Harriet Pendeniston. She would as soon have thought of falling in love with the Prince of Wales. But she had no thought of love. The romantic novels that schoolgirl Harriet had secretly devoured bore no relation to real life as she had learned to know it, and her experiences in the Cushing household had shocked her deeply. In her present state it was quite enough to worship from afar. Had she been brought into contact with some marriageable young man of her own age and social standing, she would have shied away like a startled hare. Mr Warhurst was unattainable, so it was safe to pour out upon him all the fervour of her love-starved heart. She did not even know that she was doing so as she made her innocent plans for the immediate future.

Six

Naturally enough the secret could not be kept for long. It was not even a real secret. It was just that both Mrs Bedford and Harriet nursed private qualms about Mr Warhurst's possible reaction to their little arrangement, and since it was quite unimportant neither had seen fit to mention it. Harriet had worked her way right round the book-room once before she was discovered. Growing bolder with each visit she began to spend a good deal of time in studying the sketches that she had noted on the first occasion. An in-bred notion of honourable behaviour forbade her to read the manuscript pages without permission, but one simply could not help looking at pictures. They were fascinating and puzzling, and to Harriet, who could scarcely have sketched a recognisable dandelion, their artistic merit was beyond praise. She longed to know more about them. Even to her limited knowledge it was obvious that most of the subjects were of foreign origin. Sometimes there were fragments of ruined buildings that gave this impression. Once or twice there were sketches of temples or pagodas, once a water-colour of a lagoon covered with lilies that were blue as summer skies, and in the background a strange, foreign-looking boat, vividly coloured, with awnings spread.

This was one of her favourites. There were also sketches of castles and palaces and quaint old bridges and streets, which she thought might be of European origin. She was always scrupulously careful to replace everything in its proper order, but by now she was sufficiently familiar with the various piles to go straight to her favourites for a refreshing peep to lighten her labours. She was so engaged one day when Mr Warhurst walked quietly into the room to collect some forgotten papers relating to the lease of one of the farms. He came in by the small door that had once been a postern giving on to the terraces, and Harriet, kneeling in the window embrasure, intent on her treasure, might easily have escaped his notice. But there could be no ignoring Mandy's ecstatic greeting. Harriet scrambled to her feet, flushing slightly under his enquiring gaze, and explained that she had thought him ridden out, and was just setting the room to rights.

"So I had," he said shortly, "and shall be gone again in a minute or two. But this is no fitting work for you. When I suggested that you should help Mrs Bedford, I did not mean such tasks as this. There are maids in plenty to clean and polish."

Harriet realised what Mrs Bedford had meant when she had said that for all his easy-going ways, no one would venture to take advantage of Mr Simon. His voice was still perfectly level but there could be no mistaking his displeasure. She saw the occupation that she so much enjoyed vanishing from her grasp.

"But Sir," she ventured, greatly daring. "I *enjoy* doing it. I have been bred up to work, and now that I am quite well again I cannot be happy without some occupation. Dr Fearing said that I must not sew or read for too long at a time. The furniture in this room is very beautiful. It deserves cherishing, and indeed it is not *hard* work. Besides," a little guiltily, "I rest a good deal in between whiles because I like to look at the drawings. I hope you will forgive my curiosity. I do not read the papers, I promise you, and I am very careful to put everything back just as I find it. That is why Mrs Bedford entrusted me with the task. Please say that I may go on doing it."

Her honesty pleased him, and he was not insensitive to the subtle flattery of the admiration that she expressed for his sketches, but he was not wholly appeased.

"When Dr Fearing said that you were not to sew for more than a short time," he said firmly, "I am very sure that he did not envisage you performing such menial tasks as this. You should be out in the sunshine, walking or riding. *Do* you ride, by the way?"

"A little. I was used to ride the horses at the farm, but I have no riding dress and no horse. I *have* been out this morning though, with Meg and Mandy. As for menial work, my grandmama always declared that no work done with a good heart for the comfort of a household should be so described. It was not beneath the dignity of any woman, be she gentle or simple."

Her head scarcely came up to his shoulder and there was an elfin slenderness about the childish body in its simple green gown, but she faced him bravely, her head held well up, cheeks a little flushed in her earnestness. He was mildly amused. It was rather as though that ridiculous scrap of a pug was defying the much larger Meg.

"If I permit you to have your way," he said seriously, "will you promise me that you will not neglect your health in—er—cherishing my household gods? That you will walk out of doors every day when the weather is fit?"

"I promise," she said eagerly. "An easy promise to keep, Sir, since Mandy also will insist that I keep it faithfully."

He smiled. "Then provided that you do not read for *too* long and put everything back *exactly* where you found it," he teased, mimicking her earnest explanation, "you may read any of the papers that take your fancy. They are accounts of travels undertaken years ago. There is nothing private about them, else I had not left them lying about so casually."

The small transparent face lit up with delight. Her thanks were rather jumbled and incoherent but there could be no doubting their sincerity. He gathered up his papers and left her to her innocent devices, smiling a little for her endearing simplicity and mulling over a scheme for borrowing a pony from a neighbour whose daughter was away at school. Herrington would be willing enough to lend it during Mary's absence, and a little gentle equestrian exercise would be just the thing to put some colour into his protegée's pale cheeks. She still looked to him alarmingly fragile.

He discussed this suggestion with Mrs Bedford that night when she came to thank him for giving his approval to the book-room arrangement. A very good notion, she fully agreed, but what was the child to wear? He would not have her ride astride in the boy's clothes that she had worn on her arrival. Most improper, and just the thing to set the neighbourhood talking, but to suggest the purchase of a riding dress was more than she dare do. It had been trouble enough to coax Harriet into accepting the simple wardrobe that she now boasted.

"And no use to suggest that she borrow Mary Herrington's habit, either," agreed Mr Warhurst thoughtfully. "Mary would make two of her."

Mrs Bedford waited hopefully. Her own plans were already made. Had been so, in fact, for some time. And they included more than a riding dress. It was a sensitive subject and she hoped that the initiative would come from Mr Simon if she gave him sufficient time.

So indeed it proved. "There must be stuff laid away in the attics," he said rather irritably. "Surely something from which a skirt could be contrived. If needs must she can wear her boy's jacket. But you are quite right. She must not ride astride. If word of such a proceeding came to her Grandpa Pendeniston's ears, it would be like to set him off in an apoplexy. Not that it wouldn't be a benefit to the neighbourhood, save that by all accounts his heir is worse. As matters stand she passes respectably enough as your niece, in delicate health and needing country air. At least that is the version that Jim Herrington presented to me this morning, and he seemed quite satisfied with it so I did not undeceive him. You don't object to it, do you?"

"I do not, Sir. If you and Miss Harriet are satisfied, I'm proud. And we may look in the attics for something that will serve," she reminded him tactfully.

"Of course. And if there is nothing suitable, then we must supply something by stealth. I am sure that I can perfectly rely upon you." He gave her a conspiratorial grin and then, quite suddenly, his expression sobered and he said softly, "Dorothea's things."

It was the moment for which Mrs Bedford had been waiting. She was too wise to snatch at it. She allowed quite an appreciable time to elapse before she said, "Why yes, indeed, Sir. If it would not be painful for you. Nothing could be more helpful. There must be a number of things that could be put to good use, apart from the riding dress. They would all need to be altered and shortened, of course, for Miss Dorothea was much taller than Harriet. One thing I *can* say, remembering Miss Dorothea's tender heart, she would have been the first to approve. All her sympathy would have gone out to our waif in her need. And after all, Sir, none of the family ever saw her wearing the clothes, so the sight of Harriet wearing them could not bring back sad memories."

"The memory of Dorothea could never bring sadness," returned Simon gently. "We are sorry only for ourselves, in losing her so young. Perhaps this chance-sent waif is meant to comfort us for our loss. Give her the keys to Dorothea's trunk. Tell her the story. And beg her to make what use she will of the contents."

So it came about that the next morning Harriet, a key clutched tightly in one hand, was escorted to the attics, shown a trunk, and left to make her own explorations.

Her heart was sore for her god, who had lost a beloved young sister when she was just seventeen and in the first bloom of her beauty. The wasting disease, said Mrs Bedford sadly, and little hope from the start, but one physician had suggested that a sojourn in a softer southern clime might at least arrest the progress of the fatal sickness. It was planned to send Miss Dorothea to Italy. Her trunk was already packed—and so happy and excited she had been over the dresses that had been bought for her—and then she had caught cold. No more than a summer cold, but her constitution could not stand it. Within the month she was dead. And to make the tragedy complete her mother never recovered from the grief and shock of losing her much-loved youngest child, and before a twelve-month was out she too was dead. Mr Simon had been in Germany then and it had not been thought desirable to bring him home.

What a shattering, sweeping loss, thought Harriet. Mother, sister and sweetheart, for Fiona's betrothal to his brother had been announced just before Dorothea's death. Small wonder that he had stayed abroad and had been only too content to join his father in those more distant expeditions that were portrayed in the book-room diaries and sketches.

She unlocked the trunk with an odd feeling of diffidence. It seemed an unwarrantable intrusion. Here was another girl's life, another girl's dreams. A girl a little younger than herself, who had not wanted to die since she had been happy and excited over the clothes chosen for her Italian holiday. But once she had turned back the lid, every other feeling was forgotten in rapturous appreciation of the riches that lay exposed.

After a few moments of fingering and replacing she abandoned the attempt briefly to go and ask Mrs Bedford for a dust sheet. For an attic the floor was creditably clean, but packed right on top of the trunk was a ball gown in creamy yellow silk, and the thought of putting the lovely thing down on the unprotected boards was not to be endured. Then, with a little shiver of anticipation, she began the unpacking, examining everything carefully before laying it on the dust sheet. The dresses and pelisses were a little outmoded, but since Harriet had small notion of fashion that did them no disservice in their new owner's eyes. She *did* think that some of the dresses were rather low cut, but that could easily be remedied. The skirts would have to be shortened and she could use the material to make ruffles to fill in the neck. Examining, planning, dreaming, she spent the morning in a trance, only emerging when Alice came to summon her to luncheon. Even then she must show Alice a scarf of gossamer lace, a pair of soft kid gloves and some real silk stockings before she could be persuaded to leave her treasure trove and turn her attention to the mundane business of eating.

She carried downstairs with her a round-topped coffer which she had found in one corner of the trunk. It too had been locked, but the tiny brass key was in the lock and Harriet had discovered that it contained a number of pieces of jewellery. It seemed strange that it should have been left in the trunk. Possibly the dead girl's mother had felt unable to face the painful task of going through the contents.

Mrs Bedford entirely agreed with Harriet's own view that, while she might perfectly properly accept the other contents of the trunk, jewellery was a very different matter. The coffer was put aside to be handed over to Mr Warhurst, and the pair settled happily to discussion of what could be done with the other things. They agreed that the alteration of Miss Dorothea's riding habit must be the first task. Harriet spoke wistfully of the glories of the ball gown.

"Not that I should ever have the opportunity of wearing such a gown, but it is so very beautiful," she sighed.

"You never know what the future may hold," pronounced Mrs Bedford portentously, "but there is no time for working over such luxuries as ball gowns just now. What a good thing that I did not buy muslins, since there are such a quantity, and those pelisses will be very useful to wear over your dresses when the weather turns colder. But first the riding dress."

Accordingly Alice was enlisted into service to help carry the piles of yellowing finery down to Harriet's room, where the ball gown was hung away tenderly in one of the big cupboards and piles of linens and lawns were sent down to the laundry room. Work was to begin at once on the riding dress and on two morning gowns that only needed shortening, and three days later Harriet had her first ride.

She was a little overcome when Mr Warhurst signified his intention of accompanying her on this occasion, but his prosaic explanation that he was making himself responsible not only for *her* safety but also for that of Mary Herrington's pony soon put the matter in its proper light and enabled her to exercise some control over shaking hands and a fast-beating heart when he put her into the saddle. It was fortunate that the pony was a docile beast, for she had not ridden for five years, and never in a proper habit, while the reins felt clumsy because she was wearing leather gloves. She felt very stiff and strange and was so busy dealing with these minor discomforts that she had no idea what a pleasant picture she presented, sitting very erect in the saddle with her intent and solemn face under the soft beaver hat with its pretty curling plumes.

Mr Warhurst spared her the indignity of the leading rein but he made her walk and trot and canter Dandy until he was satisfied that she had the basic skills at her command before he announced that they would take just one turn to the top of the Warren which would permit them to essay a short hand-gallop, and that that would be enough for today. Harriet, feeling more at home in the saddle with every passing minute, was disappointed, but far too much in awe of her escort to voice a protest. Perhaps he sensed this. He assured her very kindly that as it was she would feel painfully stiff after the unaccustomed exercise, and then shattered her completely by announcing that, for the moment, he meant to keep her tuition in his own hands.

"You have the makings of a capital little horsewoman," he told her, in that lazy unemphatic voice, "but at your stage it is very easy to get into bad habits. I shall not be able to take you out every day, though I should be able to manage three or four times a week until hunting begins. By then you should have progressed far enough to be permitted to ride with a groom. Until then you will oblige me by forfeiting your rides on the days when I have other engagements. I am afraid that you will find me a strict teacher, but in the years to come you may have cause to be grateful to me."

She could not possibly be more grateful than she was at this moment, thought the dazed Harriet. And she would suffer any discomforts, any mortifying strictures, rather than disappoint her teacher. It was difficult to keep her happy excitement within decorous bounds as she gathered up her long skirts with unpractised hands and hurried into the house.

Seven

A month fled. Harriet bloomed visibly. There were very few days when she did not have a riding lesson, and although, true to his word, the teacher was strict, the lessons were enjoyable because the pupil was so eager and industrious. Simon began to speculate as to whether he dare buy a mount a little more lively than gentle Dandy. Mary Herrington would want him back anyway for the Christmas holidays. Was his pupil sufficiently awake to the time of day to realise that such a mount had been bought especially for her use? He rather thought not. It was a pity, he reflected, that girls had to grow up. Fifteen—or was she perhaps a little older, he wondered vaguely—was a delightful age. He was in no mind to forego his almost daily rides. Apart from being such a satisfactory pupil, she was a pleasant companion, both sensible and intelligent. Her schooling might have been cut short, as Mrs Bedford had told him, and apart from a sweet singing voice she had no fashionable accomplishments but she had an enquiring mind and an almost masculine notion of fair play. He knew about the singing voice because these days she was so happy that she sang about the house. He knew about the enquiring mind because on their rides abroad, in the intervals of correcting her style they talked a good deal, and there were times when he was hard put to it to answer her questions. Indeed, had she been a nameless waif instead of Robert Pendeniston's grandchild, he might almost have thought of adopting her and attending to the completion of her education himself.

Perhaps that was why, when a spell of very wet weather called a temporary halt to the riding lessons, he occasionally summoned her to the book-room to discuss the journal he was writing. Harriet loved these sessions. To be asked to choose one of her favourite sketches and to be told all about it was the greatest treat imaginable. It was almost better than the riding lessons, because here her opinions were received with interest and she was closely questioned as to why she had formed them. The odd thing was that under the stimulus of her naïve interest, Mr Warhurst found his own pleasure in the journal reviving and strengthening. He had been toying with it in a desultory fashion for several years. It provided a change of occupation for the occasions when work was done, he was weary of reading and no one came to call. There were not very many of them, so the journal had made slow progress.

Now, Harriet's vivid interest brought back his own youthful memories in something of their first freshness. After she had been dismissed to her early supper and bed—on which the doctor still insisted—he would find himself sorting, editing, polishing, and completing half-finished sketches so that Harriet could get an accurate impression. The journal began to come to life in his hands and he found himself remembering a dozen half-forgotten details that must be incorporated into it. And then, of course, Harriet must be summoned so that she could hear the revised passages. His calls upon her time increased considerably, and Mrs Bedford began to grow anxious. The dealings between the pair were perfectly innocent and open, and on Mr Warhurst's part there was only a rather thoughtless enjoyment of a new interest. But where Harriet was concerned, Mrs Bedford strongly suspected that the attachment was deep and serious. And since there could be no question of marriage between such an ill-assorted pair, she was more than a little concerned. Mr Warhurst's behaviour was no more than that of a strict but kindly uncle, but she doubted if Harriet saw it in that light. Where, hitherto, she had been simply grateful for the chance that had brought Harriet under the master's protection, she now saw breakers ahead, and began to cast about in her mind for means of parting the pair. If Harriet were to fall in love with Mr Warhurst it could bring nothing but heartache. A new post would have to be found for her. Mrs Bedford judged her to be quite strong enough now to undertake some form of employment, so it be with a kindly mistress and not too onerous. She would speak to Mr Warhurst about it.

Mr Warhurst, so approached, proved singularly obtuse. He could see no need for such haste. The girl was very well where she was. In fact, she was proving unexpectedly helpful to him in his writing, as well as bringing some sort of order to the chaos that had been the book-room. Let her stay, at least until Christmas was past. It would give her time to get really strong again. After Christmas they would see.

The last thing that Mrs Bedford desired was to make her master privy to her fears. She was obliged to accept his decision and to content herself by devising tasks and errands for Harriet that would keep her away from the book-room as much as possible when Mr Warhurst was in occupation. Since she was not accustomed to such devious shifts she became unusually irritable and puzzled poor Harriet considerably.

Nor was she very successful. It was easy enough to prevent Harriet from going of her own accord to polish furniture or tidy up generally, but when Mr Warhurst sent for her there was nothing that Mrs Bedford could do except conceal her growing disapproval.

He sent for the girl after breakfast one wet day and greeted her with a teasing remark about tidying up all his papers and so making herself indispensable, since it was now much quicker to send for her than to look for things himself. Harriet blushed with pleasure, and Mr Warhurst, noting with amusement how easy it was to please her, was suddenly aware of a slight sense of shock. The child was growing up under his eyes. When he remembered the pallid pathetic scrap that he had pulled out of the river, he was amazed at the change. And while he could feel nothing but satisfaction in the obvious glow of health and well-being, he was uneasy on another count. To house a forlorn child was one thing. To shelter an attractive young woman—and for the first time, studying her with a newly-percipient eye, he acknowledged the attraction—was quite another. To keep her with him was manifestly impossible, for her sake as well as for his own.

He pulled himself together and told Harriet which papers he wanted, and she went immediately to one of the chests in the window while he considered this new complication. He had been foolish, he thought, not to realise that it would happen. Children did not stay children for ever, and Mrs Bedford had been quite right. Harriet would have to go. It was fortunate that he had realised it before any harm was done. He sighed faintly, already realising how much he would miss her.

At this point in his reflections he was interrupted by an urgent knocking on the postern door. Some one was in the devil of a hurry, he thought, and sharply bade the visitor enter. The door was pushed open violently and young Peter Pettiford stumbled into the room, breathing hard as though he had run far and fast.

"Sir!" he gasped. "Had to come. No one else to turn to. It's Jem."

It was not difficult to guess what must have happened, and when the boy had recovered his breath a little the tale was much what Simon had expected. Jem had been surprised during a poaching expedition. Of all the neighbouring estates he had chosen to favour Pendeniston Place with his attentions—and the colonel, a bitter and unrelenting foe of all poachers. Jem had not only been seen but recognised, because he had heard one of the keepers cry out that it was young Coburn, and just let the lad wait until he got his hands on him. Jem, naturally, had *not* waited. But although he had managed to give the keepers the slip, the case was desperate. He had not dared to go home and had hidden in the woods all night, making his way to the bailiff's house at first light and summoning Peter by throwing up stones at his window.

"Where is he now?"

"In your potting shed, Sir," said the boy rather shamefaced. "I daresn't let him bide at home. When they don't find him at the farm they'll come looking for him at our place."

"But they won't expect *me* to be hand in glove with the young rascal," suggested Simon grimly.

Irony was wasted on Peter. "No, Sir," he agreed simply. "That's why I thought your potting shed was the safest place. Mr Beresford is working on the long border, so he's not likely to go in, and if so be as he did chance to see Jem I don't think he'd give him away, him having done a bit of poaching himself in his time."

"And what do you expect me to do for your friend?" asked Simon curiously. "It's no use asking me to beg him off. It would take a miracle to soften the colonel's heart."

"No Sir. But I thought if you could help

him to get away." He broke off awkwardly, hesitated for a few minutes, and then went on, driven by his friend's urgent need, his eyes anywhere but on Simon's face. "You *have* helped others, Sir. And Jem's father is one of your tenants."

"So just because I have been fool enough to help one or two reckless young idiots to escape the consequences of their follies, I am to be blackmailed into lending my support to one who has already had fair warning, from me as well as from his father. And where is he to go? Young Hobbs went to his uncle in Wales, and Stapley went to the Americas. Jem is what? Fifteen? Too young to be shipped overseas. Has he any suitable relatives?"

Peter shook his head vigorously. Harriet, listening to the exchange from her vantage point in the window, guessed that he thought the matter as good as settled.

"What he wants to do, Sir, is to run away to sea," he explained confidently. "His dad would never hear of it before, but he'll have to, now, won't he? Or see Jem prisoned and maybe even transported."

"Well of all the hell-born brats!" exclaimed Simon, half-admiringly. "I begin to think the whole escapade is just a scheme to oblige Coburn to yield to the boy's demands."

"No Sir, it wasn't truly," assured Peter. "He didn't mean to be caught, but since he was, don't you think it's the best thing to be done?"

Privately, Simon did, but he explained patiently that it wasn't just as easy and straightforward as Peter made it sound. "Even if we could smuggle him away to safety—and I daresay that could be managed—every sea captain is not an honest, warm-hearted hero. The boy deserves a sound thrashing, and if he were my son he would get it, but he cannot be allowed to fall into bad hands. That could be worse than prison. No, I had best see Coburn and talk it over with him. I only hope I don't fall foul of the colonel's keepers bent on the same errand. Meanwhile, tell that stubborn young idiot to keep himself well hid, and then keep away from him. Nothing is more likely to arouse suspicion than the sight of you visiting the potting shed about every ten minutes. Yes, I daresay you will be anxious. You deserve to be, dragging us all into such a crazy start. Be off with you now. I'll do what I can."

Peter mumbled some sort of fervent thanks, and went. Simon turned to Harriet, whom the boy, in his anxiety, had never even noticed. "You heard all that?" he queried soberly. "No need to ask you not to mention it to anyone. The fewer people to know of such affairs, the safer one is. It is a little alarming that young Peter knew of my earlier dealings. I must endeavour to be more discreet in future."

He fell silent, working out how he could best approach Jem's unfortunate father in the most natural way. Some question of repairs to farm buildings, he supposed. That would give them an opportunity for private talk while they carried out an inspection.

Harriet was deeply anxious. She had been bred to cherish a healthy respect for the law of the land. It was sometimes harsh, but it had to be obeyed. It was obvious that on this occasion Mr Warhurst intended to circumvent the forces of the law and snatch away its legitimate prey. *That* must be dangerous for Mr Warhurst. She had scant sympathy for Jem, who, after all, had hurled the boot that toppled her precious Mandy into the river. She did not wish him any particular harm but she was a good deal more concerned for his would-be rescuer. At the thought of Mr Warhurst's position if he should be discovered, she felt positively sick. With a newly acquired air of maturity she said soberly, "Must you go yourself, Sir?"

Simon came out of his abstraction to grin at her indulgently.

"Indeed I must. Did you not understand that the greatest discretion is necessary? No harm will come to me, child, so take off that anxious frown. I am simply going to consult one of my tenants about repairs to his pigstyes, as is my proper duty. I can safely promise you that no officer of the law is like to lie hid in that particular vicinity in order to listen to our consultations."

She tried once more. "Is there not something that I can do to help?"

He hesitated. It was risky. But so anxious she seemed that she would obviously be better with something to do. "If you could smuggle some food to the prisoner in the potting shed," he suggested. "Mrs Bedford will give you something suitable—you may confide in her, of course. But be watchful and wary. If your first attempt is unsuccessful, do not make another. Young Jem will just have to go hungry, though I daresay he is devilish sharp-set by now. I doubt if he's eaten since yesterday."

Harriet thought it served him right, but she turned obediently to her allotted task, partly reconciled to the situation since she was to be given a small part in it. Simon went to change into riding clothes.

The plan eventually decided upon was simple enough, and after due consultation with the parties concerned it was put into operation on the following day and went without a hitch. It began with Beresford, Mr Warhurst's head gardener, making an early trip to the Coburn farm for a load of dung. Somehow a bundle of clothing and a purseful of guineas made their way back with the dung. Farmer

Coburn had thankfully accepted Simon's offer to help his lad out of the reach of the law but stoutly refused financial assistance, and regretted only that, since there could be nothing in the nature of a touching farewell, he would be unable to express his views on the boy's behaviour, which he would dearly have liked to do.

A carrier's cart called at Furzedown during the forenoon with some rolls of carpet for the bailiff's house—and left with an illegal but well concealed passenger, travelling in the general direction of Reading. The passenger was quietly deposited at a prosperous farm on the outskirts of Basingstoke, whence he passed from hand to hand among a well-disposed (but severely censorious) farming community until he reached Reading, where he took the Bristol coach, the journey having taken the better part of three days. In Bristol he met, by previous appointment, a Mr Hurst, who had received a Power of Attorney from his father to place him as apprentice to a reputable shipmaster. Jem, with all his dreams coming true, was not only a sturdy healthy lad, well fitted to strenuous undertakings, but a newly-agreeable one; an important factor in making a success of a sea-going career, as his temporary guardian did not fail to point out to him. The business was concluded to the satisfaction of all parties, and 'Mr

Hurst' was able to make his thankful way home to Furzedown once more.

The whole incident had consumed barely a week, but it marked a change in the relationship between Simon and Harriet. He had noted her developing maturity. She had behaved sensibly and helpfully during the crisis. She had shown that she could hold her tongue—though she did not spare Simon her views on the folly of involving himself with 'no-goods and ne'er-do-wells'. If he had not been in partial agreement with her, he might have been tempted to ask her into which category *she* came. Since he knew that her diatribe was prompted solely by concern for *his* safety, he abided his scolding meekly—and even in doing so furnished yet another proof that Harriet was growing up.

Eight

Mrs Pauncefoot came to spend a week at Furzedown at the end of November, upon receipt of an urgent appeal from her brother. She was a merry-faced, easy-going creature, very different from the fashionable matron of Harriet's forebodings. Her clothes were very smart indeed, but they were put on in such a haphazard fashion that she usually looked as if she had dressed all by guess. She was aware of it, strove to conquer the fault—so reprehensible in a political hostess—and finally admitted defeat, pleading to her dresser that between her husband's complicated social manoeuvres, which must be handled with feather-light delicacy, the vociferous demands of her clamorous brood and the calls of her numerous charities, she really had no time to fuss about her own appearance.

That long-suffering soul, Featherby, who adored her mistress despite the shame that she frequently brought upon her, had accompanied her lady to Furzedown and was happy to accept the services of Alice to help her unpack Mrs Pauncefoot's gowns, while the lady herself enjoyed a comfortable coze in the housekeeper's room. Mrs Bedford had been her own dear nurse and was reckoned a firm friend and ally, so the confidences that came slowly at first and then tumbled out in a tempestuous flood, were accorded their due measure of attention.

Despite her occasional outer disarray, Mrs Pauncefoot had a clear-thinking mind. She loved her brother Simon dearly, and it was her sincere hope that some day he would find in marriage the kind of happiness that she knew herself. She had tried not to bear a grudge against Fiona for shattering his youthful illusions, but she had grieved for the wasted years that followed—for so she saw them. It was more than time that Simon thought about settling himself in the world, but would this problem child that he wished to discuss with her be a help or a hindrance? She seemed to have broken through the barriers of indifference that he had erected against the feminine world, and that, at least, must be counted a gain. Further judgement she would defer until she had made Miss Pendeniston's acquaintance.

This did not prove easy. Despite her youthful seeming, Harriet had a good deal of reserve. The relationship was further embarrassed by the knowledge that the visitor was a potential employer. Her natural friendliness was curbed by the fear of appearing familiar. She spoke as little as possible and confided not at all. Mrs Pauncefoot thought her pleasant mannered but dull, and secretly rather wondered at her brother's continued interest in such a spiritless little thing. Simon's disposition must be more charitable than she had supposed.

Harriet sparkled into something approaching animation when Mrs Pauncefoot admired Mandy. She confessed ruefully that the pug had developed one or two mischievous tricks since she had come to Furzedown. She had an insatiable appetite for handkerchiefs which she filched from their owners' pockets and tore up. Harriet was currently engaged on hemming some new ones for Mr Warhurst to make good the pup's depredations. And they had not been able to cure her of pawing at doors to be let in or out, a right which she exercised imperiously to the detriment of the paintwork. To add insult to injury her patience was short, so that when you hurried to open the desired door she was quite likely to have vanished and to be making application elsewhere.

It was about the longest speech that Mrs Pauncefoot had heard from Harriet. The stiff, guarded look on the controlled little face had relaxed. In this mood, the dull child was positively pretty, decided Mrs Pauncefoot, and countered with one or two stories of the much-loved mongrel that reigned in the nursery of her London home.

She had another opportunity to assess Harriet's quality when she paid an unexpected visit to the book-room next morning. In honour of her visit the Saloon had been brought into use and she and her brother sat there in the evenings. Harriet took pains to be busy elsewhere, feeling that she must not encroach on the license already granted her, and Simon, who had hoped to see his sister forward her acquaintance with his protegée during these informal interludes, realised for the first time the anomalous position that the girl occupied in his household. Neither guest nor servant, neither child nor adult, it must at times be very awkward for her, as it was, at the moment, for him. He could not exactly summon her to present herself in the Saloon in the same easy way in which he sent for her to the book-room.

This morning, his sister breakfasting in bed, he had indeed sent for Harriet, and when Louisa made her belated appearance the pair of them were engrossed in discussion of one of Harriet's favourite sketches. Simon was making brief notes as the words poured eagerly from the girl's lips, putting in the odd question as she paused to sort out her ideas, an indulgent smile softening his mouth. Harriet did not even sense the interruption. She held the sketch at arm's length, and from time to time her eyes lifted to Simon's face. Mrs Pauncefoot, unnoticed by either of the intent pair, saw the depth of adoration lambent in the girl's eyes and, for a moment, actually shrank from a suddenly perilous situation. Mrs Bedford's fears were all too well founded. Harriet Pendeniston was fathoms deep in love with her brother. She might not even be aware of it. *He* certainly was not. But to the mature and experienced woman there could be no mistaking that look. To her credit, be it said, that her heart ached for the child, and that at that moment she made up her mind to do her best for her.

Nothing of this showed in her manner as she strolled into the room, bade the startled occupants good morning, and made one or two laughing remarks about her own idleness.

"But I *do* lead a very busy life in Town," she excused herself, "and the Hampshire air always makes me feel sleepy for the first two or three days. It is so peaceful and quiet, too, after the clamour of Town streets. You must not scold me too severely, especially as I am anxious to make a good impression on Miss Pendeniston in the hope of persuading her to come and help me with half a dozen different problems in Arlington Street."

Swift colour flooded Harriet's cheeks, and her hands flew up to her breast in an involuntary gesture of excitement. Yet at the same time she was aware of an underlying sense of desolation. Mrs Pauncefoot's visit had been planned with this very end in view. Mrs Bedford had made no bones about it. The best solution to all Harriet's problems, since obviously she could not stay at Furzedown for ever. If only 'Miss Louisa' should take a liking to her and offer her employment, she would be fortunate indeed. Now here was the golden opportunity dropping into her lap, and all that she could think of was that she would have to leave her secure haven and face the world again.

Pride came to her aid—pride and the self control learned during the years of harsh discipline. With a very good assumption of gratification she said, "Do you really think that I could be useful, ma'am?"

"I am very sure of it," nodded Mrs Pauncefoot kindly. "My family is very awkwardly arranged," she explained, making it abundantly clear with every syllable she uttered that she thought her family was as near perfect as made no difference. "I began badly by producing a girl-child instead of the expected heir, and to make amends for this lapse I had two sons within a twelve-month." She smiled reminiscently. "Quite a handful they were, but they are now at school so the thought need not depress you unduly. But then, when everyone, including me, had decided that my family was complete, I presented my husband with twins, boy and girl, now six years old. And they, if you decide to come to me, will be very much your concern, as will my daughter Dorothea. I am fortunate in having a governess and a nurse who are absolutely to be relied upon, but both are past middle age. This would not matter so much if I were able to spend more of my time with the children, but that is not possible. The introduction of someone who is young enough to play with the twins and be a friend and companion to Dorothea, seems to me highly desirable. But how to find such a person? Because obviously, in such close contact with my children, I need a person of breeding and principle. If I had possessed an indigent niece or cousin, that is the kind of girl who might have served. Which is plain speaking, my dear, I am aware, but I was never one to hide my teeth. I have no such relative, but I think that you, if you would, could very well fill the position that I have in mind. My brother tells me that you write a good clear hand and are extremely methodical, so that you could also assist me with my charitable work—well—I do not wish to appear over-eager, but I would like to have your decision as soon as possible, and if it is favourable I shall carry you off without more ado."

This frank and friendly approach was far more than Harriet could have hoped for, and there could be no question of delaying her answer. She expressed her gratitude in becoming terms that caused her new employer to nod approvingly. That lady named a salary that seemed to the girl quite excessive for such simple duties as she was required to perform, but Mrs Pauncefoot assured her that after a week or so of the twins she would discover that she was not overpaid.

"Not that they are ill-mannered or spoiled," she added, "or at least I trust you will not find them so, but they are so full of energy. I find an afternoon spent in their society quite as exhausting as one of my husband's political dinner parties.

There was only one problem to mar this hopeful prospect. What was to become of Mandy? One could scarcely expect Mrs Pauncefoot to house and feed a mischievous pup. Besides, it would be entirely contrary to established practice. Servants, even pampered ones, did not have such luxuries as pet dogs. She waited anxiously while brother and sister discussed various holiday plans in one or two of which she was included, and when they had settled all the details to their satisfaction and Mrs Pauncefoot had told her bracingly that she must get all her gear in good order to leave in three days' time, she turned to Simon.

"Will you keep Mandy for me?" she said simply. "I know it is asking a great deal. I expect I really ought to find a home for her, but this has all happened so quickly that there is no time to look about for a suitable family. I could pay you for her food—and she is always well behaved with you. Perhaps then I could see her sometimes, if we spend some weeks here in the spring as you have suggested."

Mrs Pauncefoot promptly offered to allow her to take the pup with her, but Harriet, while duly grateful, shook her head. "It would not do," she said simply. "There would be jealousy. And while I am learning my new duties I would not have time for her. No, if Mr Warhurst would keep her, just for a little while, until I grow accustomed to the thought of parting from her. You might even find a good home for her, Sir. I suppose that would really be best."

"And deprive Meg of her sparring partner? You cannot be serious! Of course I will keep her for you—and hope to teach her not to devour my handkerchiefs before you see her again. I shall not permit you to pay for her food. You may hem me some more handkerchiefs instead, for you will find that you need all your salary for clothes and fal-lals."

"Yes, indeed," chimed in his sister. "You will enjoy going shopping with Dorothea—and at last she will stop taking me to task for not providing her with a sister closer to her in age."

"I fear she will think me too old to enter into her sentiments," submitted Harriet. "Did you not say that she is just turned sixteen? Four years is a vast difference at that age."

Mrs Pauncefoot frankly stared. "Why—how old are you, child?"

"Twenty, ma'am."

Mrs Pauncefoot eyed her brother rather reproachfully. Fifteen or sixteen he had told her. To speak truth the girl did not look any more and she supposed that he had not given much thought to the matter, but it certainly did make a difference. For one thing it became more than ever essential that Harriet be removed from her brother's protection as soon as possible.

Simon, too, was startled. How could he have been so far out in his guess? To be sure the miserable starveling that he had rescued had looked far different from this composed little creature. He was thankful that his sister had taken a liking to her. It certainly solved an awkward problem. And seeing a very thoughtful expression on that sister's face, he hastened to introduce a new topic.

"And talking of fal-lals and fripperies," he said lightly, "Harriet found a box of trinkets in Dorothea's trunk—*our* Dorothea. There is nothing of great value except the pearl necklet that Papa gave her for her sixteenth birthday. Do you not think that *your* Dorothea ought to have that? Oh, yes! And the diamond bracelet that Grandmama left her. Apart from those, just one or two pretty ornaments—a locket that I gave her, and a pendant and a couple of brooches. I would like you to choose something for Harriet—you will know what would be most suitable—so that she will have a memento of our little sister when the other contents of the trunk are outworn."

Harriet's eyes glowed with gratitude, though she could not help wishing that he himself had made the choice. To a girl who had never in her life possessed an ornament, *anything* must be acceptable, but she would have liked him to finger and select. However Mrs Paunce-foot solved the problem by removing the neck-let and bracelet, turning over the other items with a casual forefinger, and then handing over box and contents to Harriet with a care-less air that entirely robbed the gesture of any sentimental significance. Secretly she was furious with her brother. Did he *want* to attach the poor child? For nothing could have been better calculated to give her a heart-ache. What between undertaking to care for her dog and pressing unsuitable gifts upon her, it was small wonder that she went about in a daze of adoration. And doubtless as soon as she had removed the poor little brat, he would forget all about her.

Simon did nothing of the kind. And no one more surprised than he. He had certainly thought to relapse into his customary bachelor comfort once the house was his own again. The brief interlude of petticoat interference had been pleasant enough, but he waved the ladies off on their journey with a certain sense of relief. Seen in retrospect the incident had been harmless and he could now revert to his old ways.

This pleasant state of mind lasted for two days. At the end of that time he began to feel uneasy. The disorder in the book-room positively irked him. The pug, Mandy, though not actually pining, looked at him with huge reproachful eyes, and he was obliged to admit that he felt restless and bored. He had lost interest in the journal and hard frost made hunting impossible. He was at odds with the world and nothing pleased him. He began to toy with a notion of going up to Town during the Christmas season. He might drop in on his sister—perhaps take his nieces and nephews to Astley's. Possibly young Dorothea was of an age to appreciate the theatre—even an evening at Ranelagh. He would see.

Nine

Thanks to Mrs Pauncefoot's skilful handling of the situation, Harriet soon fitted into the household in Arlington Street. It was generally assumed that she was a little older than Miss Dorothea since she was emancipated from the schoolroom during lessons. Mrs Pauncefoot, at first wondering how in the world she could occupy the girl, soon found her useful in a dozen different ways. With her clear writing, and spelling that was a good deal better than her employer's, it was not long before the writing of invitations and the keeping of lists and records devolved almost wholly on Harriet. Mrs Pauncefoot began to wonder how she had ever managed without her, and even the master of the house was heard to comment favourably upon her activities. She found favour, too, with the twins, because she obviously approved of their adored Tramp—an animal that appeared to be the result of a misalliance between a terrier and some kind of spaniel—and because she had a fund of stories about farm animals remembered from her own childhood and was endlessly patient with their questions.

It took longer to become acquainted with Dorothea. The girl was friendly enough, but she was at an awkward age, eager to shake off the shackles of the schoolroom, longing for the day when she would make her début. Not this coming Season, Mama had said firmly. She would be barely seventeen, and that was too young. Dorothea argued, cajoled and pleaded, but her parents stood firm. She might make an appearance in the drawing-room after dinner, and they would arrange one or two parties of younger people especially for her benefit, but there it must stop. Dorothea was rebellious and dissatisfied, and briefly inclined to be jealous of Harriet, that paragon of all the virtues, whom even Papa had praised.

Harriet was too diffident at first to take a strong line, but as her confidence in her real usefulness increased, she began to indulge in a little plain speaking. When Dorothea complained of the close watch that was kept on all her activities and excursions, not only by

Mama but by Miss Hall, her governess, and even by the older members of the household staff, any one of whom was quite likely to suggest that it threatened rain or was too cold for outdoor exercise so that some cherished scheme had to be abandoned, Harriet, while properly sympathetic, painted in the other side of the picture. How would Dorothea like to be wholly bereft of parents and friends, dependent solely on her own efforts to supply her every need? If one of her watchful guardians had suggested such a possibility, Dorothea would have been inclined to scoff at its absurdity. To Harriet, who had actually experienced the conditions that she described and who was not so very much older than herself, she was prepared to listen. And while Harriet did not disclose her more sordid experiences, she did provide an account of such an existence as gave the sheltered darling of a wealthy family a good deal to think about.

She was a good-hearted girl. Moreover she knew a little about her Mama's charitable work among the lower classes. But they had always been to her a race apart. Harriet was a girl just like herself. Indeed, her grandfather was very wealthy. Dorothea had heard Papa say that 'Old Pendeniston had shaken the pagoda tree to some tune.' The phrase had intrigued her and she had taken the trouble to enquire what it signified. It meant the acquisition of an Indian fortune, explained Mama, in accents that did not invite further enquiry. When Dorothea, greatly daring, ventured to press her, she was told that not all Indian fortunes were acquired by creditable means. There had been several quite appalling scandals on this count, which Dorothea was too young to understand. No. No one knew anything to Colonel Pendeniston's discredit, and that was quite sufficient on so distasteful a subject. Young girls should not concern themselves with such matters, and never, never mention them in public.

The fact remained that Harriet's grandfather was a wealthy man. Yet for no fault of hers he had refused to acknowledge his granddaughter. Her other grandparents were dead; her father had died before she was born. Only her mother had stood between her and the life of odious servitude which she had described so quietly and soberly. Dorothea was young and vulnerable, not without imagination. It was not difficult to put herself in Harriet's place. She found herself observing her parents with unaccustomed solicitude lest either should show signs of failing health. Partially reassured on this head by a sharp scolding from Papa for having spent all her pin money before the quarter was anywhere near done, she sought more information from Harriet, showing herself as avid as the twins in her search for knowledge.

The result was the beginning of a close friendship. It grew slowly, since there were vast gulfs of experience to be bridged between the farm-bred girl who had been carefully educated and then driven into a harsh existence as a serving maid and the cherished flower of a well-to-do family. It grew, with great advantage to both.

Mrs Pauncefoot, well aware, despite her many preoccupations, of the new docility in her daughter's disposition, and distinctly intrigued by that daughter's new-born concern for her mama's state of health, had small hesitation in ascribing this pleasing change to Harriet's influence. She had noted the improvement in the relationship between the girls, and had too much sense to pry into details. Instead she suggested that when Dorothea came down to the drawing-room after dinner, Harriet should accompany her. She knew only too well the devastating shyness that could paralyse a youngster who was the only creature present under thirty.

The suggestion worked far better than she had dreamed. In fact, not surprisingly, it was Harriet who was stiff and awkward; and in trying to set her friend at ease and draw her into conversation with ladies who, however awe-inspiring, had been known to her all her life, Dorothea quite forgot her own importance and behaved like the modest affectionate girl that she was. Her Mama was gratified to receive several compliments on her pretty unassuming manners, and when the gentlemen joined the party she dismissed the two girls to their own quarters with a soft-spoken word of praise that sent them off in high gig. She was questioned about Harriet, both frankly and obliquely, and gave, as she had decided, an expurgated version of the truth. Yes, the girl *was* Colonel Pendeniston's granddaughter. He had not approved his son's marriage and had appeased his conscience by providing for the child's education and then washing his hands of her. Since the deaths of her mother and her maternal grandparents she had been very much alone in the world. Mrs Pauncefoot had felt sorry for her and had offered her a home.

Knowing the lady's warm heart, her friends were not greatly surprised. Knowing Colonel Pendeniston in fact or by repute, they were not surprised by his behaviour either. Himself of modest if respectable birth, he had a positive passion for blue blood. He had married his only daughter to the eldest son of an earl whose sole claim to fame was an unbroken descent from one of the captains who had accompanied Norman William to these shores. The fact that this pedigree was allied to empty pockets and a vicious disposition was quite unimportant to the colonel. He had money enough to stand the nonsense and he had acquired one of the oldest titles in the land for his daughter.

She did not live very long to enjoy it—if enjoyment and not endurance was the word. She died in childbirth, leaving a son to heir both the ancient title and her father's wealth. That son was now twenty-five years of age but, by some odd quirk of circumstance, still unmarried. One would have thought him fortune's darling—well-born, wealthy and almost excessively good-looking, but for one reason or another the various noble alliances that had been suggested for him had all come to nothing.

So nobody was really surprised that the colonel had disapproved of his son's marriage to a mere yeoman farmer's daughter, though one or two rather coarse-minded dowagers suggested that such a match might have done something to improve the strain. In general there was a mild sympathy for Harriet. These haughty dames would not have welcomed her as a bride for any relative of theirs—not unless her grandfather should relent and decide to endow her handsomely—but they were quite willing to be pleasant to her as long as she did not put herself forward in any way.

That was not Harriet's intention. The varied activities of her London life had done much to alleviate a certain degree of heartache. To be sure she would wake at night and think of Mandy and Furzedown, and of Simon from whom the other two were inseparable, but she was usually so tired that she fell asleep again almost at once, while during her waking hours there was so much to occupy and to distract that she had little time for dwelling on the past.

Thanks to Dorothea's trunk she was reasonably well provided with a modest wardrobe. In Dorothea's namesake she now had a friend who was fertile in invention to cover small items that were lacking in her equipment. And unlike her friend she found the evenings in the drawing-room of absorbing interest. She listened eagerly to accounts of various parties, of plays that had been attended of a new singer or violinist who had made a successful début. There was talk of changing fashions, of Christmas festivities, even, in lowered confidential tones, or various flourishing friendships that might lead to marriage. To Harriet it was as good as a play. She said little except when directly addressed, but all the time she was studying the behaviour of others and to some extent modelling her own upon it. Her speech, her carriage, even her manners were all polished by the constant association with Mrs Pauncefoot and her friends until she began to feel perfectly at ease with them, no longer afraid of making foolish mistakes and becoming a laughing stock. Dorothea grumbled because the girls were always dismissed as soon as the gentlemen put in an appearance. Not that any of them were particularly exciting, being mostly married and elderly in the eyes of sixteen, but they *were* male. Harriet felt that she could learn far more from the ladies and was well content as things stood.

Christmas brought a relaxation in nursery discipline. The boys came home for the holidays and there were riotous games of blindman's-buff and puss-in-the-corner, in which the grown-ups joined with as much enjoyment as the small fry. Julian, the elder boy, had been given an anamorphosis. This toy consisted of a tubular mirror which was placed on a distorted picture and reflected it in its proper proportions. He and the twins spent hours gazing at this magical effect. When the weather was too wet or cold for outdoor exercise they played carpet bowls or bumble-puppy, a kind of ninepins played with a captive ball on a string. Everyone ate too much food and far too many sugar plums, and Harriet had never known so merry a Christmas.

The best—so far as she was concerned—was still to come.

Before the boys went back to school, Mr Warhurst presented himself in Arlington Street, announcing that it was high time that he became better acquainted with his nephews and nieces. His sister wondered if he had actually convinced himself that this was the truth, so boldly did he pronounce it. She was seriously put out. At any other time she would have been delighted to make him welcome. He came to Town all too rarely, but to come *now*, after appealing for her help in an awkward situation, just when Harriet was in a fair way to settling down contentedly in her new surroundings, was just the kind of thoughtless behaviour to which gentlemen yielded when some whim took them. She made no doubt that he had missed the child, running about after him as she had done, with her big worshipping eyes. So now he must amuse himself by playing the indulgent uncle to the whole brood, with whom Harriet must necessarily be included. It was quite infuriating, but she could scarcely tell him that he was not welcome!

He had come armed with gifts for the whole family, too. At least there he had shown a little more discretion. The brooch for herself, the charming fan for Dorothea, would obviously be unsuitable for a girl in Harriet's position, yet it would seem unkind to leave her out. Mr Warhurst had found what seemed at first sight to be an unexceptionable present for the girl, since it was of no pecuniary value and was just the kind of thing that one might give to a child. It was a small water-colour sketch of the puppy, Mandy, mounted but unframed. It was not until she gave rather more thought to the matter that she realised that the gift was infinitely more personal than any of the costly trifles that had been bestowed upon the rest of them. In only this one instance had time and effort been spent upon the gift. To judge by the glow on the recipient's face she would not have exchanged it for the treasures of the Indies, thought the indignant Mrs Pauncefoot. So she was unnaturally severe when her brother began to debate the various forms of entertainment with which he might amuse his young relations. Dorothea was not yet out, so there could be no question of permitting a proposed visit to Ranelagh. In any case she believed that the gardens were sadly run down nowadays. Astley's circus might be permissible, she conceded reluctantly. The twins would enjoy it of all things and so would Julian and Laurence, while if the two girls thought it a little beneath their dignity it would do them no harm to come down from their high ropes. In fact, both girls thoroughly enjoyed the treat, Harriet, who had never been so privileged before, being speechless with admiration for the ponies and their fairy-like riders, while the boys preferred the antics of Grimaldi.

Much encouraged by this success, Mr Warhurst took tickets for Sadler's Wells, where Moustache and thirteen other talented dogs recruited from the fairs of Leipzig and Dresden were playing to crowded houses in Dibdin's *The Deserter*. The clever little animals played the parts of soldiers storming a fort, until one of them ran away, was apprehended and made to face a firing squad. This affecting piece reduced Mr Warhurst's feminine guests—this time the twins were not included—to subdued sniffs. Upon mature consideration, over coffee and sweet cakes, everyone agreed that they had enjoyed the performance prodigiously, only Harriet adding the rider that, while filled with admiration for the performers, she preferred her dogs to behave naturally.

"Mandy and Meg," she tried to explain, "are intelligent and *wise* rather than clever. They have been taught obedience and good manners and then they teach themselves the engaging little ways that endear them to their owners. I should not like Mandy to be drilled like those performing dogs," she concluded firmly.

The twins were less squeamish. They raised such riot and rumpus over being left out of the Sadler's Wells visit that their uncle very handsomely made amends by engaging the Punch and Judy man to come to their very own house. Even so they exacted their pound of flesh, insisting on seeing the whole piece twice through and clapping gleefully when Punch was arrested by the constable, magnificent in his tricorne hat, and an officer in a cocked hat with a cockade and a long pigtail. The boys, with Dorothea and Harriet, counted themselves too grown up to condescend to such a juvenile form of entertainment, but it was to be noticed that they did not make this discovery until the man had packed away the puppets and taken his departure.

All good things, even school holidays, come to an end. The halls of learning reclaimed Julian and Laurence, both vowing that it had been the best holiday ever and that Uncle Simon was a regular trump, an opinion confirmed by the guineas surreptitiously slipped into each ready palm at the moment of departure. Uncle Simon himself was obliged to made his adieux, since the next meet was to be at Furzedown and he must be there to play host. Life in Arlington Street settled down into its customary routine. A certain watercolour sketch graced the mantelshelf in Harriet's bedroom, and it is to be regretted that when, at bedtime, she studied it with loving concentration, her gaze was apt to focus on the corner where the artist had scribbled his initials rather than on the liquid brown eyes that looked out at her so soulfully.

The only person who was not entirely satisfied was that regular trump and generous benefactor, Mr Simon Warhurst. He did not know quite what he had expected. Everything had gone splendidly. His nephews and nieces were a pleasant set of young people and he had enjoyed their enjoyment, but something had been lacking. Perhaps the visit had been too short. He wondered how soon he could persuade Louisa to bring the girls to Furzedown for a visit.

Ten

Since Mrs Pauncefoot had no intention of doing anything so ill-judged, he was destined to become increasingly frustrated. He learned that it was not desirable for Dorothea's studies to be interrupted again so soon after Christmas, and that in any event the weather was too inclement to favour a sojourn in the country. When the fine days of April rendered this excuse ineligible, the situation was saved by the twins, who developed chicken-pox. Their harrassed Mama, realising that she would shortly be pressed to take them down to Furzedown for a period of convalescence, could only be thankful for the intervention of Lady Preston.

Lady Preston was a firm friend, one of Mrs

Pauncefoot's charitably minded associates. She had been absent from the London scene for more than a year, visiting old acquaintances and more particularly her two sons who were both stationed in India. Mrs Pauncefoot welcomed her joyfully and the two ladies enjoyed a comfortable gossip during which Lady Preston enquired affectionately after her friends the twins. They must, she suggested, have grown out of all recognition. Their mother described their indisposition—actually a very slight one—and went on to outline her plans for Dorothea's come-out next year, mentioning incidentally the young companion who had exerted such a beneficial influence on the girl.

Lady Preston pricked up her ears. "Did you say Pendeniston?" she demanded. "Colonel Pendeniston's granddaughter? Let me see now. What did they call the child? Mary named her for her father, I know. Henrietta, was it?"

"Harriet. Do you know her?"

"No, but I knew her mother, and held her in considerable affection. When Robert died and I came home to England I tried to get in touch with her, only to discover that she had died some time previously and that the farm where she had lived had changed hands. No one seemed to know what had become of Mary's daughter. Her brother had left the district and I assumed that he had taken the child with him. If it is the same girl I would dearly like to make her acquaintance. Her mother was with me in India when the boys were small. A tower of strength. I would gladly do her daughter a kindness for her sake. Is she entirely dependent on her own efforts? It seems to me quite incredible that even Colonel Pendeniston could be such a monster as to cast her off."

"Harriet says that he *did* provide for her schooling. And there seems to be some suspicion that her uncle made off with funds that were rightfully hers, but she is an independent little thing and will not hear of appealing to her grandfather for further assistance."

Lady Preston nodded thoughtfully. "In that respect at least she resembles her mother," she commented. "I think that it was Mary's sturdy independence as much as her lovely face and pretty ways that appealed to Henry Pendeniston. He needed someone to support him against his old curmudgeon of a father. Mary might have managed to have put some spirit into him if he had lived. I shall look forward to meeting her daughter."

Under these auspicious circumstances the acquaintance flourished. Lady Preston, intelligent and widely travelled, knew better than to force the pace. She studied the girl carefully, assessing her quality before broaching the subject of her mother. She was pleased with what she found. Harriet had a gentle dignity that was very becoming. She was eager to please, but content to remain quietly in the background until her services were needed or her attention claimed by one of her companions. A nice-looking child, too, though not so pretty as her mother.

When she claimed Harriet's notice and spoke to her of her mother, this good impression was endorsed. Harriet forgot her carefully acquired composure, flushing and stammering as she answered the gentle questions, her love for her mother very evident in the eager pride with which she spoke of her. To the suggestion that they must have a really long talk together, she returned a delighted assent.

"If Mrs Pauncefoot can spare me, I would dearly love to hear all that you can tell me about my mother. You are very kind."

It was arranged that she should spend an afternoon at Lady Preston's house and take tea with her. She was a little shy at first. The house was luxuriously furnished with many oriental touches that gave it distinction. In Arlington Street the schoolroom wing was shabbily comfortable, the drawing room elegant but severe. Here there was a touch of opulence, a richness of colour that Harriet found attractive but strange. Her hostess was well accustomed to meeting all sorts and conditions of people and very soon put her at her ease and had her talking quite frankly and freely of her situation. She even told this kindly creature who had known her mother the whole sordid story of the Dorset episode and of how she had run away and been rescued. And Lady Preston listened and asked the occasional question, studied the changing expressions in the unguarded face that was raised so confidingly, and read a good deal between the lines, understanding better now the slight reserve with which her friend had spoken of Harriet's difficulties. It was obviously desirable to set a distance between the girl and her rescuer. Louisa could not be blamed for setting her face against that sort of entanglement. Much the best thing that could be arranged for Harriet was a suitable marriage. If she could be brought out—in a modest sort of way, of course—it might be possible to find her a husband. The alternative was a lifetime spent in other people's homes, serving them in whatever capacity they demanded. And they might not all be so kind and considerate as Louisa Pauncefoot. What the girl needed was a sponsor. Someone who would take her about and put her in the way of meeting some eligible young men. To be sure she had no money, but her birth was respectable and Lady Preston suspected that with proper dressing and a little encouragement she might well turn into something of a honey-pot. There was a good deal of personality behind the quiet exterior, and a good deal of intelligence, too. And if—admittedly it was a big if—a creditable marriage could be contrived for her, surely the colonel would furnish some sort of a marriage portion, if only for his pride's sake. When Harriet had been patted and kissed and dismissed in her ladyship's own carriage to Arlington Street, Lady Preston began to consider ways and means.

By the following day her decision was made. She herself would sponsor Harriet. She did not anticipate any difficulty in persuading Louisa to resign the girl to her care. In fact, if she had read the situation aright, her friend would regard the offer as an excellent solution to a delicate problem. The only slight difficulty might lie in persuading the girl herself to acceptance. Lady Preston trusted to the strength of her old acquaintance with Harriet's mother. If she could convince her that her Mama would have fully approved the course she suggested, the battle would be won. And she could truthfully add that there was nothing she would enjoy more than having a temporary daughter to take about with her, to dress and to cosset.

It would be well to put the scheme into being as quickly as possible, she decided, and set out at once to pay a morning call in Arlington Street. Here, as she had confidently expected, her suggestion was greeted with enthusiasm.

"She is a dear, loveable child," declared Mrs Pauncefoot, expansive in her relief, "and

I shall miss her sorely, but there can be no denying that she has conceived a girlish adoration for Simon—scarcely surprising under the circumstances—and that he is inclined to be amused and flattered by her devotion. No more to it than that, I promise you, but it must be nipped in the bud, and that is so difficult when the conduct of both is quite above reproach. The only thing I could think of was to speak to Simon—ask him not to encourage the child—you know the sort of thing—but I feared to make too much of the whole business. This scheme of yours is so very much better. I am sure she will forget all about her ridiculous tendre for Simon when such a wonderful opportunity is presented to her. And when she meets other gentlemen she will come to see that he is by far too old for her. She is a very fortunate girl to have found so kind and generous a friend."

Harriet found herself in a state of bewilderment. She was young enough to feel a lift of the heart at the thought of the treats in store, wise enough to realise that this could only be a temporary arrangement and that it might have to be paid for with a painful return to the workaday world. Not that either Mrs Pauncefoot or Lady Preston was likely to cast her adrift entirely, but no one, however kind, could be expected to support her in idleness for ever. Something of this she tried to explain to them, but it was not easy to make her point clear without being unpleasantly blunt, and this she could not bring herself to do. At the kindly suggestion, intended to allay her fears for the future, that she might contract an eligible alliance if she were given a fair chance, she shrank instinctively, not quite knowing why, and said stiffly that she had no mind to marriage. Lady Preston, remembering the story that the girl had told her, thought that she understood, and the subject was allowed to drop.

"Then we will find you a pleasant post as companion to a lady—such tasks as you have performed so satisfactorily here. But first you will grant me the indulgence of pretending for a little while that you are the daughter I never had," she went on persuasively. "I feel sure that your own mother would be willing to lend you to me, do not you?"

It was a powerful argument, but the real clincher was delivered, quite unintentionally, by Mrs Pauncefoot. One could hardly decline an advantageous and attractive offer and say that one would prefer to remain in one's present employment, when one's employer was bubbling over with enthusiasm for the new scheme and busily suggesting new ideas. To be sure she dutifully bewailed her personal loss, vowing that her friend had robbed her of a treasure, but she made it very plain that she expected Harriet to accept without hesitation. Against her better judgement, Harriet yielded.

Once committed, however, she threw qualms about the future to the winds and gave herself up entirely to enjoyment of the present. She had liked Lady Preston from the first. The terms in which that lady had spoken of her mother had strengthened that liking. It was not long before she realised that all the business of grooming her for social success was of absorbing interest to the older woman. In that respect at least, she comforted herself, she was of some use, for her pride still choked occasionally on the bounty that she was obliged to accept. Lady Preston said, very reasonably, that there could be no point at all in skimping the business and was inclined to be over-generous, while Harriet, with no experience in the needs of a young lady moving in fashionable circles, was shocked at the extent of her indebtedness. It didn't stop with the provision of a suitable wardrobe. There were dancing lessons and singing lessons, and a horse must be hired from the livery stables so that Miss Pendeniston could ride in the Park. But as the days passed, Harriet became accustomed to her hostess's impulsive generosity and learned to accept gracefully when some charming trifle was pressed upon her. She drove out with her ladyship to pay numerous calls, during which she was introduced as "Miss Pendeniston, the young friend who is spending the summer with me." Invitations began to arrive in which her name was included with Lady Preston's, and she was bidden to practice her dancing assiduously. Dorothea helped her here, coming daily to step out the various figures with her under Monsieur Rambouillet's careful instructions. She went to the theatre, where she was wholly entranced by the gaiety and vivacity of Mrs Jordan, and to several concerts and an exhibition of paintings. Her manner was still rather subdued. She had a great deal to learn and it would be very easy to make a mistake and bring ridicule not only on herself but upon her sponsor, but her confidence was growing with every fresh hurdle surmounted, and Lady Preston noted with quiet satisfaction the steady improvement in her appearance. If she could have seen the girl that Simon had pulled out of the river, she would have been even better pleased. The months of sheltered living, the good food, and the society of people who had her welfare at heart, had done their work. Harriet's hair was still only a loose curly crop, but it had regained the sheen of health. Her skin was clear, her colour good, and there was animation in glance and voice. A modest social success, one or two complaints, a few floral tributes and an occasional flirtatious glance, and the thing would be done. The girl would glow into a beauty all the more appealing because it was a subtle thing, a compound of colouring and expression rather than the standard blonde prettiness or a brunette magnificence.

She began to plan a party for her young guest. Not a set ball, she decided, but a dress party with dancing and cards for the older guests. Nothing too ostentatious. No more than fifty or sixty invited. She wondered if Louisa would permit Dorothea to attend. It would not be a popular suggestion since Louisa was always so insistent that the girl was not yet 'out', but her friend's support would be a great comfort to Harriet on so important an occasion, and surely Louisa owed her something!

Reluctantly Louisa acknowledged this. Careful enquiry eliciting the facts that all the guests were known to her; that no young gentlemen of the fortune hunting persuasion were included in the list, and that on *no* account would the waltz be danced, she agreed that Dorothea might attend. She herself would chaperone her daughter and they would leave early to emphasize Dorothea's schoolgirl status.

Lady Preston immersed herself happily in an orgy of preparation. Even for so small a party, everything must be well done. The wines and refreshments must be of the highest quality, the musicians skilful and not too obtrusive, the floral decorations of original design. To be sure she had never given precisely this kind of party before, but she had done a good deal of entertaining during her husband's official career and she anticipated no difficulty. Nor did she encounter any. The only flaw in the arrangements was the choice of Harriet's dress. At twenty turned she was not obliged to wear white, and both ladies were agreed that the paler pastel shades were more becoming. But if the colour was right the fabric did not drape well, while in certain cases the cost of the materials was so excessive that Harriet simply could not like them. Lady Preston was almost in despair, for time was fast running out, when Harriet said hesitantly, "I know what I would like to wear for our party, if only you would consent to it." She did not dare add, "And it will cost us nothing," for that argument would never serve to persuade Lady Preston to agreement. Instead she said shyly, "I have been in love with it ever since I first set eyes on it, and if I could wear it I am sure it would bring me good luck. It is the ball gown that I found in Dorothea's trunk. Do let me show you. I believe you will like it as much as I do."

"But I cannot let you appear at your own special party in a made-over gown," protested Lady Preston.

It was the reaction that Harriet had expected. "I know it seems unusual," she said soothingly. "But the dress has never been worn. It is not as though any one would recognise it, and in any case it would have to be altered into a modern style. It is the material that is so beautiful. Do, pray, let me show you."

Lady Preston's air of patient tolerance vanished at the sight of the gown. As the girl had claimed, the material was exquisite. They had seen nothing to touch it. It was a soft brocade, not too heavy for a girl, but firm enough to hold a line. The basic colour was a pale straw-gold, and it was brocaded with white daisies, lightly tipped with coral. It was youthful without being juvenile and it set off Harriet's delicate colouring to a nicety. Lady Preston capitulated forthwith, declaring that Harriet's dress sense was developing nicely and summoning her maid to discuss how best the brocade could be altered.

The days grew ever busier. Harriet went to breakfast parties and boating picnics. She drove in the Park with her ladyship and rode with Dorothea. She attended a gala performance at the Opera, where Lady Preston pointed out all the notabilities. She made the acquaintance of a group of young people who were pleasant and friendly and entertaining. There was little chance of these acquaintances developing into close friendships because the groups were always shifting—breaking up and re-forming just as one seemed to be approaching intimacy. Harriet enjoyed it all to the full—and felt exactly as though she was taking part in a play. So far she had performed her part very creditably and she looked forward eagerly to the scenes that were still to come. It did not do to spend too much time in speculating as to what would happen when the play was done. Dutifully she wrote out invitations, stood to be fitted for her party dress, went shopping with Lady Preston's maid for gloves and slippers, and began to acquire the art of keeping at a distance certain young gentlemen who seemed eager to fix their interest with her. She liked them well enough. It was pleasant to be guided through the intricacies of the dance by an arm stronger than Dorothea's and she enjoyed such small customary courtesies as having a glass of lemonade brought for her when she was hot and thirsty, doors opened for her, a chair found. But she did not care for having her fingers pressed in significant fashion and had no desire at all to seek the seclusion of sheltered nooks in garden or conservatory in order that a few words might be exchanged in private. Such attentions drove her back immediately to Lady Preston's side. And while that lady could not disapprove such decorous conduct, she could not help wishing that her charge would offer a little more encouragement to one or two perfectly eligible gentlemen who were showing signs of interest in her and who had *not* shied off, despite the knowledge, delicately conveyed by her ladyship, that her protegée had no expectations. Of course there were still several weeks to go before people began leaving Town. Perhaps the party would help matters on. The sight of Harriet in her new-old gown might be expected to have a devastating effect on gentlemen already well-disposed towards her.

Eleven

Mr Warhurst was surprised but on the whole well-pleased to hear of the change in Harriet's situation. He liked the thought that she was enjoying herself and hoped that Lady Preston had dealt with her independent notions more successfully than he had done. He did wonder rather anxiously what was to become of her when the Season ended. It would not be easy to go back to servitude, however easy the conditions, after a taste of the life she was leading now. The possibility that she might marry never entered his head. In his view she was still not far removed from the puny child whom he had pulled out of the river. When he had been in Town he had noticed with approval that she was growing to be quite pretty, but he kept forgetting that she was also quite grown up and still tended to regard her as one of the schoolroom party. He wondered what she was making of her new fashionable life and, remembering the way in which she had brought life to his literary labours, thought that he would dearly like to hear her own account of her experiences.

Come to think of it, why should he not spend a few days in Town and do just that? There was nothing urgently requiring his attention at home. He remembered that he had been contemplating the purchase of one of the new phaetons. Apart from his travelling chaise he had never bothered much with carriages, preferring to ride except on long journeys. Recently he had found himself thinking that it might be pleasant to be able to tool Louisa about the lanes. One might even teach Dorothea and Harriet to drive. Yes. He would take a run up to Town and look in at Hatchett's.

With this laudable object in view he descended on his sister on the day before Harriet's party, apologising for not informing his surprised relations of his intentions and begging his sister not to put herself out. If it was inconvenient for him to stay in Arlington Street, he would seek shelter at a hotel. The sorely tried Louisa assured him, with a slightly artificial smile, that of course it was convenient and that he was very welcome, but regretted that she would see very little of him as she had engagements that she really could not cancel. He accepted this cheerfully, explaining his real reason for coming to Town, which afforded her some measure of reassurance, and adding that he would probably look in at his club and catch up with the talk of the Town.

All might have gone well if Mr Pauncefoot had not chanced to be spending one of his rare evenings at his wife's tea-table. "Better idea than that," he announced jovially. "You can take my place at Lady P.'s party tomorrow. You'll do the pretty far better than I would—handsome young fellow and a bachelor to boot—and I shall be able to get down to the House after all."

Since Mrs Pauncefoot had been at considerable pains to coax her husband into attending the party with her, she was justifiably annoyed at this base desertion. She suggested that it was discourteous to say the least, just the sort of casual behaviour that her husband deplored in the rising generation—and then spoiled it all by adding that Lady Preston might take offence.

"Not she!" declared her husband roundly. "Best-natured woman alive—except you, of course, my dear," he put in hastily. "I'll just send her a note, telling her there's an important Division on, and she'll understand right enough. And happy to accept my substitute, I shouldn't wonder." He directed a conspiratorial twinkle at Simon and ambled off to his library, there to plunge into the complicated plans that were the breath of life to him, and to forget all about matters domestic.

Simon was a little diffident about accepting his brother-in-law's suggestion, since, although he had heard a good deal about Lady Preston, he had never actually met her. He admitted to a certain curiosity concerning the lady, and when he learned that the party in question was being given in Harriet's honour, his scruples vanished, though he made a decent pretence of protest.

His sister said crossly, "Men! You have no consideration at all. When I think of all the trouble that we have been put to—but there! Talking pays no toll. I suppose you and Gerald will have your way."

Mr Warhurst was a little puzzled. He really could not see that Louisa had been put to any particular trouble. And she was in general the most easy-going and tolerant of females. Eventually he ascribed her ill-humour to Gerald's defection and set himself to make soothing conversation about his nephews and nieces until he had won her back to a more equable mood.

He spent an enjoyable—and expensive—day, next day, visiting most of the establishments in Longacre and eventually choosing a phaeton, a real high-flyer, a shapely crane-neck which, with all the extra refinements that he decided upon would cost him well over two hundred pounds, and returned to Arlington Street feeling well disposed to all the world and in ample time to change into his evening rig—the new one that he had ordered at Christmas when he discovered that long-tailed coats were now all the crack. He studied it critically, as also the richly embroidered waistcoat that went with it, and fancied that it made him look taller. At any rate he would not disgrace his family by appearing in rustic guise, and for once he was actually looking forward to the kind of social gathering that he would normally have been at some pains to avoid.

Lady Preston's house was admirably designed for parties of moderate size. From a central hall the staircase rose in wide, shallow steps to a gallery shaped rather like a lozenge, the two principal rooms leading off to left and right, three beautifully proportioned arches facing the visitor as he mounted the stairs and leading to smaller reception rooms and the service staircase. There was no ballroom proper, but the drawing-room, stripped of most of its furnishings, could comfortably accommodate half a dozen sets, while the smaller rooms provided space for the card players and a well-furnished supper-room. With staircase and gallery banked with roses and brilliantly illuminated by carefully disposed groups of candles in silver holders, the scene was both festive and welcoming. Simon followed his sister and Dorothea up the stairs, marshalling in his mind the words that should express his gratitude for Lady Preston's kindness in permitting him to substitute for his brother-in-law. For a moment or two he did not even see Harriet, absorbed in his first meeting with his hostess, trying to sum up her personality from voice and appearance. Then she presented "Miss Pendeniston" to his notice—and he realised that the lovely, glowing girl who was standing beside her was 'his' Harriet.

There is a great deal to be said for a strict training in social behaviour. Patterns of conduct become so much second nature that a dazed mind seeks refuge in clinging to them. Neither Simon nor Harriet could ever afterwards remember what they had said on this notable occasion. Presumably nothing startling or outrageous, since there were no gasps or curious stares. Certainly the gentleman asked the lady for a dance, since his name was later to be found inscribed on her programme, while the lady's pretty blush and brilliant eyes were possibly the result of a very natural excitement. Not even the watchful Mrs Pauncefoot suspected that the civilities that Harriet proffered to the guests who followed them were purely mechanical, or that her eyes saw only a tall, beloved figure in a well-cut tail coat, his unpowdered head easily distinguishable among those who clung to the older fashion. Nor did any of the ladies who exchanged polite small talk with the handsome Mr Warhurst—what a pity that he was so seldom seen at such gatherings as this—catch an echo of that inner voice that reiterated clamorously, "My darling. My little love. Oh! What a fool I have been. What a stupid, purblind fool. Pray heaven it is not too late."

It is to be regretted that Harriet gave a considerable degree of encouragement to her several admirers from her own sheer happiness. There was no time to think. She had read the startled admiration in Mr Warhurst's eyes, and it had awakened her to the full knowledge of her femininity. What the future might hold she neither knew nor cared. Tonight she was beautiful, admired, desired. Tonight she would dance with Mr Warhurst. With Simon, she ventured, shaping the name soundlessly. Who cared for tomorrow?

Instinct—or education—had served Simon well. He danced only once with his Harriet, and, indeed, danced rather stiffly and awkwardly, so intense were his feelings at seeing her swing and dip and turn her head at his ordering. But it was the supper dance, and although they exchanged little enough conversation and in any case their neighbours could overhear every word, they were together. They could exchange glances as Simon told of Mandy's assumption of matronly dignity now that she was a full year old, a dignity that lapsed regrettably when she scampered after Meg down a rabbit track. Once Simon's arm brushed Harriet's as he re-filled her glass with Lady Preston's champagne cup. They were both ridiculously, idyllically happy.

Idylls, alas, are short-lived. Supper over and a long spell of duty dances ahead of him, Simon's mood was less rapturous. He found it difficult to avert his eyes from the undoubted triumph that Harriet was enjoying. It was not surprising. She was adorable. He just wished that her admirers would content themselves with adoring from a distance. She made a delightful picture as she danced and smiled and chatted with partner after partner. It was not until he noticed her dancing for the second time with one particularly devoted looking gentleman that he began to feel uneasy. At first he could not think why, for it was perfectly proper to dance twice with the same partner though anything more would be regarded as fast. In fact, it was not for some time that he pinned down the reason for his discomfort, and by then Harriet had danced with several other gentlemen. He found himself disliking them all equally. It was not just ordinary jealousy, he realised. It was the fact that they were all so young. His attention once drawn to this circumstance he looked further, only to discover that with one or two exceptions he was by far the oldest gentleman on the floor. It struck him, too, that none of the young sprigs of fashion who were performing with such enthusiasm were known to him. He began to feel that despite his elegant attire and his proficiency in the figures, he was old fashioned and out of place. From that it was a very short step to the realisation that he was too old for Harriet. As he danced and bowed and paid mild compliments with affable grace, he was calculating. From what Harriet had said she must be close on twenty-one. And he was thirty-one. Almost thirty-two. Half as old again. To be sure he knew of marriages where the disparity of age was even greater, but he doubted if they could be described as happy ones. And for Harriet he wanted only the best.

To his credit be it said that none of his partners noticed his preoccupation. In fact, had he but realised it, he scored a success that almost equalled Harriet's. There were whispered enquiries as to his identity and history from such maidens as had not had the privilege of an introduction, bright eyes measured him from beneath demurely lowered lashes, and more than one languishing glance was directed towards him. He performed his duty faithfully. It would have been almost a relief to retire early when his sister took the reluctant Dorothea home, but his hostess urged him to stay and in view of her kindness it was the barest courtesy to consent. He joined a set of quadrilles with a child who could not have been much older than his niece, and was thankful that he was obliged to attend to the figure in order to avoid disgracing himself. At least the exercise provided some distraction from his miserable thoughts.

He had no further private conversation with Harriet. When he came to render his thanks to Lady Preston, her charge was engaged with a group of lively young people arranging some pleasure party for the following day, and he insisted that she should not be called to bid him farewell. In his heart he had, alas, already bidden her farewell.

He puzzled his poor sister considerably next day. She was warily prepared for any suggestion that he should take Harriet and Dorothea on some perfectly unexceptionable outing that would yet be highly undesirable. He made no such suggestion. Instead he told her that he rather thought he would look in on Erridge and Fiona if they were still fixed in Town, and then he would be off back to Furzedown.

"Though I may drop in on you again in a week or so, when I come up to Town to collect my new carriage." And went on to describe the vehicle's manifold perfections as though he had no other care in the world.

His sister gave it up. She would never understand men, she decided. Or perhaps she had been making much ado about nothing. Apart from commenting that Harriet had looked very becomingly and had appeared to be quite at home in society, he evinced no particular interest in the girl. He repeated his pressing invitation to his sister to bring her family to visit him. Since obviously this invitation no longer included Harriet, Mrs Pauncefoot took this as further evidence that his interest in her had died a natural death, and thankfully dismissed it from her mind.

While Simon, having paid a long overdue visit to his brother's Town house and exchanged polite small talk with the languidly lovely Lady Fiona and her harassed-looking spouse, set off for Furzedown in a mood far different from the cheerful anticipation of his journey to Town, Harriet was wondering shyly if she might expect a call from him. The rapturous mood that had enveloped them both at supper still lingered. She was not quite sure what she expected. Nothing had been said but the rapport between them had been unmistakable, even to the inexperienced Harriet. A great many gentlemen had called this morning to pay their respects to Lady Preston and to thank her for last night's hospitality. It seemed only natural to suppose that Mr Warhurst might also do so.

The morning wore on to afternoon, and they were engaged to attend a military review, and still Mr Warhurst did not put in an appearance. Perhaps he would come tomorrow she thought, rather disconsolately, and went to change her dress.

The military review brought her a new and distinctly intimidating acquaintance. They were about to climb into the carriage for their return when an elderly gentleman in a very neat curricle pulled up his horses and attracted Lady Preston's attention. She recognised him at once. But it scarcely needed her hissed, "Your grandfather," to apprise Harriet of the gentleman's identity. Somehow she had expected him to look just as he did—neat, spare and ill-tempered.

His voice matched his looks. It bit like a saw.

"Lady Preston, ma'am?"

Even that was an assertion rather than a question. Her ladyship bowed politely. Harriet was pleased to note that she was not in the least discommoded by the abrupt address.

"Sir?" she responded.

He wasted no time on courtesies. "You may permit me two minutes conversation with this young woman, if you will be so good," he said stiffly.

Lady Preston smiled sweetly at Harriet.

"Are you willing to let bygones be bygones and to acknowledge your grandfather?" she said gently, and succeeded only in discomposing Harriet. The colonel was quite unmoved. Harriet's colour rose, and since she could think of nothing polite to say she contented herself with the smallest of curtsies.

"I am grown weary of rebuffing the enquiries of the curious," said Colonel Pendeniston with an air of chill indifference. "Insolent persons who scarcely know me appear to feel it incumbent upon them to enquire whether the Miss Pendeniston who is making some stir in fashionable circles is indeed my granddaughter. It will be convenient to have the facts established beyond conjecture. I have decided that you had better spend a week or two at Pendeniston Place during August. Bring your maid. She can act as chaperone. I will instruct my housekeeper to have rooms prepared for you."

He inclined his head, said, "Servant, ma'am," to Lady Preston, and turned away as though there was no more to be said.

Twelve

There was, of course, a great deal more to be said. The circumstances of her upbringing had moulded Harriet into a reasonably docile creature, and when Mrs Pauncefoot and Lady Preston had both shown her such kindness it went sorely against the grain to run counter to their advice. But did they really expect her to submit meekly to her grandfather's dictum and go and stay in his house? From all she had heard of it—and since it lay only three or four miles from Furzedown she had heard a good deal—she had as soon go to prison. She told them bluntly that she felt herself under no kind of obligation to her grandfather. Even the money that had paid for her schooling had not really been of *his* providing but had come from his wife's estate. Perhaps if he had been frail in health or alone and friendless she might have felt more kindly disposed towards him. As it was she could see no reason why she should accept his invitation. It would be more accurate to say why she should bow to his command, for his instructions had been given so coldly and impersonally that no one could imagine that he had any real desire for her presence. He himself had said that it was purely a matter of convenience. He wished to put himself right in the eyes of the world.

Her two advisers were obliged to concede all this, but were far more conscious than was Harriet herself of the advantages that could accrue to a girl whom the colonel was prepared to acknowledge as his granddaughter. He was not a likeable man, but great wealth can do much to make a man acceptable to his fellows. If the colonel could be persuaded to provide a marriage portion for Harriet, together with the protection of his name and a settled home of her own, Lady Preston and Mrs Pauncefoot could forgive him a good deal. They tried to persuade Harriet that his cold speech and autocratic ways stemmed from long years spent in India with far too many servants obedient to his lightest whim.

Harriet stood firm. She would be grateful for the help of her friends in seeking a new post, but she would not go to Pendeniston

Place. The last weeks of the Season were upon them, nothing had been arranged about her future, and to make matters worse she had received two offers of marriage and had declined them both. Even kind Lady Preston scolded, and said she was an ungrateful improvident chit, and then wept, which was worse. Harriet soothed and petted her, admitted that it was very bad, and agreed that either Mr Repton or Mr Wilbraham would have made her a kind, comfortable sort of husband. It was just that she didn't want to be married.

That, alas, was untrue. She did very much wish to be married, but the man on whom her heart was set was far above her, and if she could not have him she would rather go single all her days. Once or twice, when the distractions of her fashionable existence failed her, she had turned wistfully to the memory of the dance and the supper that they had shared on the night of her party, and had wondered how she could have been so completely mistaken in her reading of the situation. She had been so sure that he liked her; that he thought her pretty. So sure that he would seek her out again, and soon. He had not done so. His thanks for hospitality received had been written in a polite note which Lady Preston had handed over to her to read. He had not even called when he came up to Town to collect his new phaeton. True, he had only stayed a night or two. She had heard of the visit quite casually through Dorothea. She supposed that one should not expect dreams to come true in real life. He had been kind and generous and had helped her to a more comfortable way of living. No doubt he was thankful enough to be free of any further responsibility for her. To imagine, even tentatively, that he might like her well enough to desire to make her his wife, had been the height of folly. After all, at several of the parties that she had attended, she had seen the woman whom he *had* wished to marry, Viscountess Erridge. She had not cared for her a great deal, thinking her languid manner affected and suspecting that she had been spoiled by an over-indulgent husband, but she was very lovely, even if something of her beauty derived from the attentions of a skilled lady's maid, and she was unmistakably an aristocrat, blue blood in every vein of her slender, fine-boned body. Poor Harriet, only too conscious of her own humbler birth, had thought that she was like the princess in a fairy-tale. She might not be very much use in an every day existence, nor as a comrade in arms in time of trouble, but she was just the kind of dream creature that a gallant knight expected as the reward for his endeavours. Harriet was just too young and too serious to feel sorry for the knight when he woke up to reality.

Matters moved to a crisis when Lady Preston received word from her sister-in-law, also a widow, residing in Bath, that she was in poor health and very low spirits. The poor health was the aftermath of a severe attack of the jaundice. The sufferer was mending but was still weak and sickly. The poor spirits were caused by the behaviour of her daughter who, rejecting all her Mama's efforts to get her suitably riveted, was determined to pursue a career in supervising the education of young ladies, following in the footsteps of the distinguished Mrs Trimmer. The unfortunate parent could not imagine how she had come to produce such an unnatural child, and felt that a visit from her sister-in-law, so sensible and so cheerful, might help to bring her misguided child to her senses and would certainly help to elevate her own spirits. Lady Preston was naturally anxious to respond to this pathetic appeal. After all the excitements of the Season, a month spent in the more leisurely atmosphere of Bath would be very much to her taste. But what was she to do with Harriet?

She was too kind to point out to the girl that she had become something of an embarrassment but she was quite unable to restrain herself from discussing her sister-in-law's predicament. Since the Pauncefoot family, with the exception of Papa, was going to Worthing for the month of August, it was plain to a sensitive girl that there was only one place for her and that was her grandfather's home. It made no difference that both her friends suggested that she should accompany them, to Bath or to Worthing respectively. Her presence could add nothing to their comfort and might, indeed, stretch accommodation already limited to the point of *dis*comfort. With a sick heart—for it hurt to be superfluous—and a composed demeanour, Harriet announced that she had decided after all to go to Pendeniston Place.

She was overwhelmed with approval and offers of support. Not only was she following the course of conduct that her friends had sincerely advocated for her own good; it also chanced to be the one that best suited their present convenience. Mrs Pauncefoot offered the use of her light chaise to convey her to her destination. Lady Preston volunteered the services of her invaluable Benworthy as dresser and chaperone during the all-important visit, declaring that she could perfectly well dispense with the good creature during her vist to Bath. Once assured that Benworthy was very willing to fall in with this suggestion, regarding it rather as a challenge, Harriet was only too thankful to accept. She had a suspicion that familiar friendly faces would be at a premium in Pendeniston Place.

The suspicion proved to be well fancied. The atmosphere of rigid propriety began at the gates, which were closed and locked. Quite an imposing gateway, with a solidly built stone lodge enclosing it on either side and impressive armorial bearings carved above the central arch. So far as Harriet was aware the Pendenistons were not entitled to bear arms. Presumably this was her Cousin Vernon's badge. Studying it—she was afforded ample opportunity of doing so by the slow and ponderous folding back of the heavy gates—she could see that the carving was of fairly recent date.

Despite this early intimation of rigidity, the Place itself gave a pleasant impression. It was not over-large, soundly built during the Jacobean age, and intended as a comfortable family home. Unfortunately, its present owner's idiosyncrasies had been so severely impressed upon his servants that it was conducted with a formality more suited to a palace, and the pleasant homely air was lost. No one smiled. Indeed the servants rarely raised their eyes beyond a point situated some few inches in front of Harriet's breast, to which they addressed all necessary information. She was luxuriously accommodated in a suite of rooms that overlooked the rose garden, its furnishings and hangings of the first stare and an atmosphere that dared her to leave a thing out of place. She found herself tiptoeing about the elegant parlour, starting nervously at the tiny sounds that drifted in from the garden. Nothing more alarming than two gardeners at work, she saw with relief, and wondered what she had expected. She scolded herself for growing fanciful but the sense of discomfort persisted. The house and its inmates appeared to be waiting in taut expectation for some coming event.

Her grandfather had greeted her with more civility than she had expected from her first impression of him. He actually expressed the wish that she might enjoy her stay and regretted that there were no other young people staying in the house with whom she might pass her time. This state of affairs would be remedied within a few days, when her cousin was expected. Meanwhile, he trusted that she would be able to amuse herself in strolling about the grounds or with such needlework or sketching as she favoured. One of the grooms had been appointed to attend her if she wished to ride and a carriage would be at her disposal if she preferred to drive. She would not, of course, set foot out of doors without the attendance of maid or manservant.

Harriet knew that such restrictions were quite commonplace in the upper echelons of society. She might have guessed that her grandfather, with his obsession with all matters of rank and pedigree, would be a high stickler for rigid formality, and while she was a guest under his roof she could hardly ignore his wishes, but she had never been so bored in her life. Once or twice she ordered the carriage, but there was nowhere in particular to go, and she knew none of the neighbours, and to be turning out a carriage and pair, a coach-man, a footman and her maid in order to drive one unimportant girl in aimless fashion about the dusty lanes struck her as impossibly pompous, while the business of locking and unlocking the gates behind her each time the carriage passed through them began to get on her nerves. Lapped in luxury as she was, needing only to ask to have her least wish gratified, she felt as though she was imprisoned. She could not help comparing the Place with beloved Furzedown, where gates stood open all day long unless some farmer was moving stock along the lane and the animals had to be dissuaded from browsing over the flower beds. Wistfully she wished that she could have had herself driven over there—see dear Mrs Bedford and her precious Mandy. But such a visit must inevitably present the possibility of a meeting with Simon, and after the hopes that had sprung up in her heart at their last meeting, only to perish so miserably, *that* she could not endure.

The air of expectation that she had sensed, even in the decorous elderly servants, was intensified on the day that her Cousin Vernon was expected. Harriet herself was aware of a certain degree of anticipation. After the deadly monotony of the past few days, even a fresh face would be stimulating. Moreover her cousin was young. Surely he would not be so eaten up with pride of race as was her grandfather. He would be someone to talk to, to ride with, or play cards. He might even prove to be a sympathetic companion. After all, a cousin was the nearest thing to a brother. She went down to dinner with some hopes of pleasant diversion, having heard the sounds of arrival while she was changing her dress. Even Benworthy suggested dressing her hair in one of its more elegant Town styles. "Though if I may drop a word in season, Miss, you'll be on your guard with the young man. Very wild, I've heard tell. Not that any one here says a word against him. To be sure they don't say many words about anything. Never known such a close-mouthed lot. But if you'll forgive me, Miss, being as how milady said I was to keep a special eye on you, you not having a mother to warn you of possible danger, it's a funny thing that there's not a young maidservant in the house. Footmen, and lads in stable and kitchen. No girls. It could just be that the young man's a bit of a rake, and the colonel's taken precautions accordingly. I hope I'm not exceeding my duty in speaking so plain, but I couldn't reconcile it with my conscience to keep mum."

Harriet reassured her anxious attendant and promised to be very circumspect, though it seemed unlikely that even the most dissolute rake would attempt to seduce her under her grandfather's roof. In fact her first impression of her cousin was quite pleasant. He was, as she had been told, extremely good-looking, his colouring dark, his features classically perfect. Tall and rather slender in build he was dressed in the height of fashion. Indeed a more experienced woman might have thought him a trifle over-dressed for a quiet family dinner in his own home. Certainly Mr Warhurst had never dressed so fine. Cousin Vernon's voluptuously embroidered waistcoat was magnificent to behold, even if Harriet vaguely felt that it would have been more appropriate on the stage. Mrs Jordan had worn one very similar in the part of Sir Harry Wildair.

In contrast to his pleasant appearance, Cousin Vernon's manner was cool. He was perfectly polite, said all that was proper on first meeting so close a connection, and, when prompted by his grandfather, took his share in an exchange of civil small talk throughout dinner. Yes, indeed, there were some very pretty bursts of country quite close at hand, and it would be his pleasure to show them to his cousin. He was pleased to hear that she preferred riding to driving, since the preference matched his own. At this point Colonel Pendeniston threw in an unexpected caveat.

"Very well so," he grunted, "but none of your neck or nothing tricks when you're riding with your cousin. I don't want either of you brought home on a hurdle."

Harriet was surprised. She had not suspected him of such human warmth.

Cousin Vernon smiled, a trifle frostily she thought. "Nothing of the sort, Sir," he assured. "I shall take the utmost care of my cousin, I promise you."

The colonel did not seem quite satisfied. "See that you do," he said gruffly, and intimated to Harriet that he and his heir would join her in the drawing-room after they had drunk their brandy. Harriet, who had never before found herself in the rôle of the hostess who gives the signal for the withdrawal of the ladies, was positively grateful for the hint, finding herself in real charity with her grandfather for the first time.

Only her cousin came to join her in the drawing-room, their grandfather, he said, having business to attend to that would not keep. His mood was now remote, almost surly. Had he been twenty years younger she would have suspected that he had been spanked and told to mend his manners. As it was they exchanged platitudinous views on the London Season and discussed the possible direction in which they might ride next day until the tea-tray was brought in. No point in waiting for Grandpapa, announced Cousin Vernon. He was engaged in dealing with some poaching threat. So Harriet poured the tea for the two of them and was thankful when it was drunk. Far from proving the congenial companion and possible ally that she had hoped, her cousin showed signs of adding to the tensions that already burdened the atmosphere of the Place. It was with a sense of relief that she bade him goodnight.

Thirteen

They rode together next morning. It did not take Harriet long to decide that a solemn progress attended at a discreet distance by a stolid groom was much to be preferred to riding with her cousin. Not that she actually *did* ride with him. He left it to the groom to put her up, did not wait to see her comfortably settled, and was urging his own mount to a gallop before they were well clear of the stable yard. Since the mare that her grandfather considered suitable for a lady was a placid creature of sluggish habits, she was left far behind. Not that she had any ambition to emulate her cousin. When she caught an occasional glimpse of him he was either spurring his unfortunate horse to greater efforts or putting it at obstacles that must, she felt, procure a crashing fall. When she finally came up with him as she turned stablewards once more, she was not surprised to see that the poor brute was going dead lame, nor that her cousin was still in the saddle. He was not the kind of man to seek to ease the animal's suffering.

At luncheon he put in no appearance. Her grandfather supposed that he had ridden over to see friends in the neighbourhood and then proceeded to question her as to how she had enjoyed her morning ride and what she thought of her cousin. She prevaricated as best she could, saying that she had thought Cousin Vernon a very daring horseman and much above her touch, and assenting when asked if she did not think him extremely good-looking. Her replies seemed to please her grandfather, who sounded almost affable as he announced that he had felt sure that the cousins would deal extremely together.

She spent a very dull afternoon with a book in the garden, her thoughts wandering all too frequently from the printed page to dwell anxiously on the problem of her future. She wondered how much longer she would be obliged to endure this tedious existence and whether Lady Preston had as yet set out for Bath, and racked her brain for the hundredth time for some scheme which would permit her to earn a modest living independent of charity. Dinner was rendered uncomfortable by her grandfather's assumption that her stay would be a long one, and by the way in which he linked her activities with her cousin. He seemed to believe that they were now on friendly terms and would be well able to entertain each other without further effort on his part. Cousin Vernon's distaste for this prospect became more and more pronounced as the meal wore on. Harriet wondered that her grandfather could remain so oblivious. If it had not been so rude it would have been funny. But she really did not see why she should put up with her cousin's yawns and the occasional scarcely veiled sneer, and she decided to take the first opportunity of acquainting him with this opinion. When Colonel Pendeniston, sounding for once almost urbane, informed the young people that they might withdraw to the billiard room, Harriet, who had never learned to play billiards and had certainly no desire to learn from such a tutor, made no demur.

Neither did she make any attempt to select a cue from the rack negligently indicated by her companion, but took up an erect stance on the hearth, looking surprisingly militant for one so slightly built.

"It will save us both a deal of time and patience, Cousin, if you will accept from the outset that I have no intention of making any claims on your companionship," she said, rather tartly, perhaps, for of late she had not been accustomed to gentlemen who spurned her society. And when he did not immediately answer, she added for good measure, "I had rather spend the hours alone than seek society so grudgingly given and so ill-suited to my tastes."

There was an odd gleam in the dark eyes that surveyed her so indifferently. "So you were not a consenting party to the old man's plan. At least, Cousin, you have succeeded in surprising me. And it will be my delightful duty to enlighten you as to his intentions. If you knew him as well as I do, you'd have guessed there was something devilish havey-cavey about him buttering you up the way he did. This is it. You are selected for the supreme honour of becoming my bride."

Harriet gasped and choked. Her eyes widened incredulously. For a moment she thought she could not have heard aright, but there was something oddly convincing in the cool distaste writ plain on the aristocratic features. Her hands went back against the rough stonework of the chimney breast. It was solidly reassuring.

"You are serious?" she said quietly.

"Would any man jest over such a business?" he countered.

She thought about that for a moment, then said slowly, "Grandpapa must be mad."

He gave her a queer, twisted little grin,

seeming in that moment more human than she had seen him. "*Merci du compliment*, Cousin," he murmured, "but I assure you that he is perfectly sane. Unfortunately, he cherishes certain old-fashioned notions. One of them is a fixed determination that his heir—myself—should marry and beget a son. Since he holds the purse-strings he is in a position to enforce the first part of this delightful scheme."

"But why me? We scarcely know one another. And surely he could look much higher for a suitable match for his heir."

He bowed ironically. "Your modesty is quite refreshing, my dear. To be sure he could. In fact, he did, not once but several times. But thanks to certain small activities that I initiated in self-defence, it was found impossible to get any of these favoured females up to scratch, which is why the privilege has fallen to you."

"But *you* surely do not imagine that I would consent?"

"Why not? You have no prospects, and no other family to support you. It seems to me that you do pretty well out of the business."

Harriet could only stare. Such monstrous conceit was impenetrable. It was with difficulty that she kept her voice steady as she said, "I shall not thank you, milord, for an offer that I regard as an insult. Only let me make it plain to you that nothing would persuade me to accept."

He flushed darkly. "Very heroic," he said. "Wait until you have experienced Grandpa's notions of persuasion. Remember that he is legally your guardian, since you are not yet of age; that you placed yourself in his care of your own free will. A week or two locked in your room on bread and water and a sound whipping every day will soon teach you to sing a different tune. After all—what have you to lose? Let me tell you at once that you need fear no importunities from me. I do not care for women. My tastes lie in other directions. I shall not object to your taking a lover, so it be done discreetly, though I'll not let you foist some other man's brat on me. If you get yourself into that sort of tangle you will have to take one of these long holidays abroad that are so fashionable among the smarts."

Harriet felt sick. After her experiences at the Cushing's and the lewd talk that she had heard among the servants there, she had thought herself immune from the kind of shock her cousin had just given her. His cold, unconcerned decadence was new in her experience. Never again would she willingly touch his hand, and the thought of being married to him, even on the terms that he suggested, filled her with revulsion. But somewhere within her a warning voice was sounding. He seemed to desire this marriage, even if it was to be a hollow sham. For financial reasons, he had said. And he had spoken of his grandfather's persuasive methods. If both men were set on accomplishing this infamous business, she stood in grave danger. She had only Benworthy to turn to, and what could a servant do against two determined men? Somehow she must make her escape from the Place before her relatives realised how utterly detestable she found their scheming. What she must do now was to play for time.

Loathing the necessity, she forced face and voice to tranquillity as she said thoughtfully, "At least I shall give myself time to study the proposition. Your arguments, milord, are powerful."

"Now that is being sensible," he told her approvingly. "And you name another argument. I can ennoble you with a title. You will like that."

Harriet thought that any association with her cousin could only degrade her, but it was no part of her plan to tell him so. She murmured something noncommittal about being unaccustomed to such exalted circles.

He nodded condescendingly. He might not like females, but he had not cared for the suggestion that one of them should reject the opportunity of marrying him. This humble creature would serve his purpose very well. He would ensure that his grandfather settled ample funds on him before the knot was tied, and no nonsense about money in trust for his heir. The girl could stay at the Place, though he had no particular objection to her going wherever she wished, so that she did not interfere with him. *This* bride had no influential relations to take him to task for neglecting her. She would do very well. She could even have the use of the Town house, since he did not like it above half, preferring something more intimate. In fact it might be better if she *did* take over the Town house. One might as well keep the old man quiescent as long as possible, and it would be easier to simulate normal married life if they had an establishment of their own. There would be squalls enough when the desired heir failed to put in an appearance, but provided that they were not all living under one roof he could always put the blame on the girl.

Mulling over these comfortable thoughts, he was too absorbed to notice any stiffness or artificiality in his cousin's behaviour. Which was fortunate, since she had had little practice in the art of feigning. She had said that she would think the matter over and he was in no doubt as to the conclusion that she would reach. It was natural that she should appear a little subdued when such important changes were about to take place in her style of living.

Colonel Pendeniston was less gullible. Apprised of the interview that had taken place in the billiard room, he was less certain of the ultimate outcome. So far as he knew, his granddaughter had no friends in the neighbourhood to whom she could turn for advice or help, with the exception of Warhurst of Furzedown, who had placed her with his sister. The risk of her turning to him must be accounted negligible, but the colonel was a thorough man. At dinner he regretted politely that he must limit the young people's freedom of movement for a few days. There was an epidemic fever in the village and he must ask them to confine their expeditions to his own acres until such time as all danger of infection was past. If Harriet had been inclined to believe this invention, the faint smile on her cousin's face would have been sufficient to convince her of its falsehood. She knew something of the sensations of a terrified hare crouching in its form, wondering where to run for safety.

If anything had been needed to convince her that she was virtually a prisoner, it would have been supplied by her cousin's conduct when they rode together next day. It had seemed to her injudicious to decline to ride with him, and ride she must, since she hoped to discover some means of escape. She had a little money. Not very much, but sufficient, she thought, to pay her fare on the stagecoach to London, where she could surely find

find some employment. If she could only discover where the coaches stopped. It would be at an inn, where they could change horses and refresh the passengers, but she dared not risk asking her cousin and he never let her out of his sight. Punctiliously he reminded her of his grandfather's warning, putting a hand on her rein when she would have turned in the direction of the village, and presently asked her if she had as yet come to a decision on the vexed question of matrimony.

"I am naturally impatient," he bowed, with a smile that struck Harriet as purely evil.

She summoned up what courage she could and declared that she would not be hurried, but her heart was cold with fear at the sight of his amused shrug and she knew that she must make her attempt at escape before her freedom of movement was still further restricted. She spent the afternoon in strolling about the garden, endeavouring to present the appearance of a maiden meditating a momentous decision while all the while her eyes were darting from side to side seeking some means of escape from this luxurious trap. There were two places where it might be possible to break out of the grounds into the lane that joined the highway. One was dangerous—too close to the lodge and the locked gates—but she thought the other, by way of a tree to the orchard wall and then into a water meadow, might be achieved without detection. The difficulty would be in getting out of the house after dark, for the colonel and his myrmidons were meticulous about seeing that all doors and windows on the ground floor were secured, and while a scramble over a wall was one thing, she could not see herself getting out of her bedroom window by way of knotted sheets. She would have to take Benworthy into her confidence and see if the maid knew of any means of egress that would serve. From experience she was well aware that servants often had their own means of defeating over-strict employers.

It appeared that Colonel Pendeniston's indoor servants were not of this calibre. Benworthy, shocked by the tale poured out to her while she dressed her young mistress for dinner, was only too anxious to be helpful but knew of no breach in the defences. Harriet went down to dinner no nearer to breaking free from her prison, and over dinner the atmosphere became so strained, with the colonel no longer affable but decidedly snappish, that her fears increased to a point at which it became difficult to behave normally. She was truly thankful to escape to her own rooms without having him ask point blank for her consent to the iniquitous marriage that he proposed to make for her, and knew that such a confrontation could not be long delayed.

Benworthy was waiting to put her to bed, a Benworthy agog with secret excitement, so that she delivered her news in a hissing whisper as she undid hooks and unbuttoned sleeves.

"There's to be a door left open tonight, miss," she confided. "The colonel's going out after poachers again. Nobody's supposed to know except Jamieson, because the colonel always suspects the underservants of being in strings with the village folk and sending warning to the poachers. Which I'm sure no one would blame them, but when the master goes out he uses the little door from the morning room on to the terrace, and Jamieson leaves it open for him to come back. It would be easy enough to get from the terrace to the orchard. The moon will be up, but not too bright."

She did not trouble to explain how she had come by this information, the truth being that she and the middle-aged butler had struck up a very promising friendship, and that Jamieson had seen no harm in imparting to this pleasant visiting abigail the secret that he was pledged to keep from his underlings. Harriet did not think to question her. She was too busy deciding what was best to be done if only she could escape from the sleeping house and thence by way of orchard and meadow to the lane that led towards Alresford. Escape by night ruled out the possibility of boarding the stage. There might *be* a night coach, but she had no idea when it was due and she certainly could not endure the strain of waiting, perhaps for several hours, in such close proximity to her enemies. There was no help for it. The only safe refuge was at Furzedown, four miles away. She could walk that, easily. Simon would receive her kindly, she was confident, and suggest somewhere for her to hide. In only two more weeks she would be twenty-one. Then her grandfather would no longer have the power to lock her up and ill-treat her. She would be free to make her own way in the world, and if the prospect seemed a bleak one it was at least infinitely better than the one that her grandfather and cousin had planned for her.

It was fortunate that Benworthy had been given a little slip of a room next to Harriet's. They arranged that she should keep watch to make sure that the colonel had set out on his punitive expedition. If she was seen she would make the excuse that her young mistress was restless and that she had come downstairs to warm some milk for her. Harriet put up a fervent prayer that her grandfather's projected route did not lead in the direction of Furzedown, and awaited Benworthy's summons with what patience she might.

She had dressed with some care for her perilous venture. Plain dark clothes were an obvious common sense measure for one who wished to be inconspicuous, and light town slippers would not do for walking four miles through the woods. Partly from sentiment she chose the simple green dress that Simon had bought for her, ignoring the fact that it was now distinctly tight, and telling Benworthy airily that she might be glad of its warmth if the night air struck chill. The buckled shoes that had come with the dress were the only ones she possessed that were in the least suitable for the expedition, and over all went a brown hooded cloak that had been Mrs Bedford's parting gift to her when she left Furzedown. It was foolish fancy, no doubt, but she felt braver in those clothes, as though she was protected by kindness and affection.

It was past two o'clock before Benworthy crept into the room to call her, and she had gnawed her knuckles sore in her growing anxiety. Well she knew that there would be no second chance. If she failed tonight, she would be so closely guarded that her case would be hopeless. She crept though the silent corridors on Benworthy's heels, scarcely daring to breathe, starting whenever a board creaked under her tread. But nothing moved. Benworthy let her out of the terrace door, promising in a whisper to feign utter stupefaction over her disappearance and wishing her well in her journey. She could not do better than entrust herself to Mr Warhurst's hands, she added hearteningly. A proper gentleman, that one.

Treading softly down the terrace steps, eyes and ears alert for anything that moved in the half-dark, Harriet only wished that she was already safe in that kindly care. She was obsessed by the fear that she would run upon the party of gamekeepers headed by her grandfather and be hauled ignominiously back to captivity. The tree and the orchard wall could not be surmounted without a certain struggle and flurry, but still nothing else moved. She breathed a little more easily when she dropped down into the meadow and began to make her way to the stream that she meant to use as her guide. It would mean rough walking, but at least she would be moving by hidden ways, with ample opportunity to take cover if danger threatened.

It took her longer than she had expected. She saw no one, but the moonlight was treacherous and she had to watch her footing carefully. Despite her urgent need to reach shelter, it would do no good to turn an ankle. Dawn was already at hand as she climbed the gate that led to the stable-yard at Furzedown. She did not wish to rouse the household. With memories of the reprobate Jem, whom she had helped succour, she contemplated hiding in the potting shed until the house began to show signs of life. Surely, then, knowing its ways as she did, it should be possible to slip quietly indoors and make her way to Mrs Bedford.

She had reckoned without Mandy. As she passed the corner of the stable buildings where the dogs slept, there was an outburst of shrill barking, supported and sustained almost immediately by Meg's deeper bay. Her attempts to quieten the pair only made matters worse, Mandy, upon recognising the beloved voice, going into a perfect ecstasy of yelps and whines and whimpers, hurling herself against the door and generally behaving like a creature demented.

Since Simon was the only one who slept in the old end of the house nearest the stables, he was first to hear the uproar, and after waiting for a moment or two in the hope that the dogs would settle down again, he got up, pulled on a dressing-gown and went to investigate, expressing his views on these disturbers of his peace in distinctly colourful language, since he suspected that the cause of all the excitement was no more than a marauding rat. He turned the corner of the building explaining aloud just what he would do to the sinners when he laid hands upon them and stopped short at the sight of the small figure pressed against the door. For a moment he thought he must be dreaming. Then she abandoned her vain attempt to quieten the dogs and turned towards him, her face bleached and strained in the pale light, her hands outstretched in mute appeal.

"Harriet!" he said softly. "My dar—my dear child! What brings you here at such an hour?"

Fourteen

Explanations were impossible until Simon had found the key and let out the excited dogs. Only when Mandy's hysterical greeting had calmed was it possible for the two to hear each other's voices. Simon, watching Harriet cuddle the small wriggling body against her breast, saw the tears drip on the soft fur. Something was desperately wrong to bring the girl here, alone, at this hour of the day. He had left her safe, cherished, with a woman who had seemed genuinely attached to her. What had happened to send her running to him? And thanks be to God that she *had* run to him.

He took Mandy from her, tucking the protesting little animal under his arm, taking

Harriet's elbow in his other hand and steering her towards the familiar small door that gave access to the book-room.

At the sight of the room where she had spent so many happy hours, the tears flowed again, but Harriet had reached her longed-for haven and was soon scrubbing her cheeks vigorously and apologising in shamefaced fashion for her foolish weakness.

"It is just because I have been so frightened," she explained simply, "and now that I know I am safe the silly tears *will* come. There wasn't time before."

Simon studied her silently, taking good note of the marks of strain in the pale little face, a long rent in the cloak where she had torn it climbing over the wall, and the soaked and muddy shoes.

"Are you hungry?" he said pleasantly.

Harriet looked startled. She had expected him to enquire immediately into the reason for her unexpected arrival and had been trying to arrange her thoughts to answer him. But now that he mentioned it, she realised that she was very hungry indeed, having eaten little at dinner the previous night.

"Yes," she said baldly.

"Then I'll raid the larder and see what I can find. Meanwhile," he poured wine into a glass and set it on a small table by the chair in which he had installed her, "drink this. Every drop. And keep that wretched animal quiet or she'll raise the house." For Mandy was still voicing her rapture in a series of crooning whimpers punctuated by an occasional sharp 'yip'.

For the moment it was enough to be here, hugging Mandy, sipping her wine, Simon bringing her something to eat. Simon would know what she should do, she thought contentedly.

Simon certainly knew how to feed a hungry girl. He brought ham sandwiches which he shared with her, thick slices of plum cake and a dish of new season's apples, apologising for the lack of coffee because it would take too long to light the kitchen fire but proffering instead a glass of rich, creamy milk which had stood overnight in the cool dairy.

It was just as well that she felt much stronger and steadier after she had partaken of these delicious viands, for Simon, when she poured out her tale to him, was frankly horrified.

It took some time to convince him that her own relatives had actually conceived such a disgusting scheme. In fact, it was the active assistance of Benworthy in such conduct as must cause any well-trained lady's maid to hold up her hands in horror, that finally persuaded him that Harriet had not permitted imagination to get the better of her. If Benworthy had considered that flight was essential, this was no girlish green-sickness.

Slightly ashamed because he had actually doubted his love, Simon said crisply, "Knowing the circumstances under which you fled, this is the first place where he will seek you."

Unaware of his temporary disloyalty, Harriet said cheerfully, "But not just yet. There is plenty of time for you to devise a hiding place. It is not for so very long. In two weeks time I shall be of age, and he will no longer have any control over my actions."

Simon could not help delighting in her trust, but the business was not so simple as she seemed to think. She was young, female and pretty. Sooner or later she would be missed, and people would want to know where she had been. Unless a credible tale could be devised her reputation would be sadly blown upon.

That would have to be thought about, he decided, but not now. It was already five o'clock. In another hour the servants would be about. Soon after that Harriet would be missed. He must have her away to a place of safety before the hunt was up. All other considerations must wait upon that prime necessity.

As though her thoughts had chimed with his, Harriet said, "Could you not smuggle me away as you did Jem Coburn? I don't want to bring trouble upon you so I don't want to be found here. But if we could get away now, before people are astir, I could hide in the woods until you have time to make arrangements for me like you did for Jem."

"My dear girl, if I were to drag you all over the countryside as I did young Jem, I might succeed in putting your grandfather off the scent but I should be equally successful in arousing the curiosity of a great many other people. Charming young ladies do not drive about the countryside with gentlemen unchaperoned. Nor do they ride in carrier's carts or stage coaches, while the respectable yeomen who sheltered the reprobate Jem would be shocked to the core by such hoyden behaviour."

This was a severe setback. The thought of the way in which Jem had been spirited away from his enemies had done much to keep Harriet's courage high during the anxious hours of the night.

She said slowly, "Why should I not cut my hair and wear boy's clothes? I daresay Mrs Bedford still has Horace Cushing's suit tucked away somewhere, and I have some money left so you could buy me a shirt once we have put a distance between ourselves and the pursuit."

He stared at her thoughtfully. It was a possibility. For himself he did not see how any one could possibly mistake the bewitching little face and charming figure for anything but feminine, but people were surprisingly unobservant. A little judicious padding on the shoulders and no opportunity allowed for close inspection, and the trick might hold. No cutting of that pretty hair though, just as it was regaining its natural beauty. It could be dressed in horizontal curls over the ears and a neat little queue at the back, with a tricorne to make the wearer look more masculine. Boots might help, too, and all these items could be purchased without difficulty once they were away from the immediate neighbourhood with its danger of recognition. He began to think quite kindly of Harriet's suggestion and to work out the essential details.

"They are bound to send here to enquire for you," he planned swiftly, "and I must be here to answer them. Everything must be open and straightforward and I shall invite them to search where they wish. I'll have you away to the Coburn's farm within the hour. You can stay there until the coast is clear. As you know, the Coburns have no cause to love your grandfather, so you will be safe with them. I will come for you as soon as I have allayed suspicion, and will bring such articles of disguise as I can lay hands on. But where I am to take you then poses something of a problem, since the places that spring most readily to mind will be the first to be searched. However, that is a matter that will keep for the time being."

Harriet spent a long and anxious morning in Mrs Coburn's apple room, where the board shelves were all scrubbed and fresh ready for the new crop and the scent of former harvests still hung on the air. Only her hostess knew she was there, Simon having planned their arrival for a time when the maids were busy in the dairy and poultry yard and the men in the fields. She had nothing to do but pace up and down the little room, peeping occasionally out of the dormer window that overlooked the farm-yard and growing more and more sleeply. In the middle of the morning Mrs Coburn panted up the narrow stairway with a glass of milk and a plate of ginger biscuits and the reassuring news that no one had come enquiring for her. Eventually she drifted off into cramped, uneasy slumber, curled up on the floor, her head uncomfortably pillowed on the window sill.

Simon pursued his normal morning avocations, save that he told Mrs Bedford that he would be away from home for a few days and asked her to have a bag packed for him. For all his calm and idle seeming there was tense expectation within him. Until he had dealt with the expected interview he could not plan ahead and it was close on eleven o'clock before 'Cousin Vernon' put in an appearance. One of the maids came to the book-room to inform him that a Lord Halford had called and asked to see him on a matter of urgent business.

Mr Warhurst was polite but distant, a busy man interrupted in the midst of his preparations for a journey, identifying his caller as

'Colonel Pendeniston's grandson' whom he had not previously met, and enquiring how he could be of service.

Cousin Vernon displayed no particular embarrassment in disclosing his predicament, saying that he and his cousin had had what he described as a lover's tiff. The girl had refined too much upon their difference—Mr Warhurst would know the exaggerated notions that females could take into their heads—and had run off. He and his grandfather were much concerned for her safety. Had she, by any chance, sought shelter at Furzedown?

It was beautifully, gracefully done, the 'concern' permitted to show through the easy mask, the rueful acceptance of a girl's whim. If Simon had not already heard Harriet's account he might have been deceived. As it was he had no objection to telling one or two thumping lies if it seemed desirable, and certainly none to making the fellow squirm a bit if it could be done.

"You amaze me," he said tranquilly. "The last time I was in Town Miss Pendeniston seemed to be settled with Lady Preston and enjoying a considerable success. I was not even aware that she had taken up residence with her grandfather. Not that it is any affair of mine, of course, but it must have been a very sudden decision. While as for a match being arranged between the pair of you, I find that even more surprising. Lady Preston and my sister listed an impressive array of suitors for your cousin's hand, but yours was certainly not included among them, and that is no more than a month past. If already you are so far at outs that your betrothed is driven to flight, one wonders if you would not be well advised to think again. First cousins, too. But so it always is with such confirmed bachelors as myself," he added sweetly, before Cousin Vernon could enter a protest. "We are always ready with advice. You must forgive my cynical approach."

Eventually he managed to dispose of the caller by suggesting that he should search the place as thoroughly as he wished in case the runaway had sought shelter unbeknownst to any one, offering the services of his household and bidding Mrs Bedford enquire most strictly among the servants as to whether any of them had seen Miss Pendeniston, but excusing himself from taking part in the search on the grounds that he was just making ready to leave. The only thing he regretted was the deep distress evinced by Mrs Bedford on hearing that Harriet had disappeared. He comforted himself in the knowledge that it would be short-lived, and that in her ignorance she had done Harriet invaluable service. None of his careless evasions would be by one half so convincing as poor Mrs Bedford's woe-begone face.

It was Mrs Bedford, in fact, once Cousin Vernon had taken himself off and her anxiety had been allayed, who suggested a possible refuge for Harriet. A friend of hers lived just outside Chippenham, where the Bath road turned off. The two met rarely but had corresponded for years. Mrs Bedford was sure that Miss Wilsher, a retired governess and the pink of respectability, would agree to shelter Harriet for as long as was necessary. In fact she would write her a note which Mr Warhurst could deliver in person. No one would think to look for the fugitive there. Only it might be better if Harriet was to change back into her own proper clothes before presenting herself, since Miss Wilsher was a trifle stiff in her notions and might not take kindly to a young lady gallivanting abroad in boy's dress.

All these instructions Simon presently delivered to his charge, together with a bundle that contained Mr Horace Cushing's suit and a neat plain shirt, together with a pair of boots, a tricorne hat and a driving coat which would at least serve to make it more difficult to identify the wearer as female.

Refreshed by her nap and with all present care removed by Simon's presence, Harriet was in tearing spirits, delighted by her own appearance in masculine guise as revealed in Mrs Coburn's mirror, practising the dashing swing with which she would sweep the drab coat about her shoulders and fiddling with her hair in a way which Simon pointed out must inevitably betray her sex. That made her behave with more circumspection, and presently she had her revenge, for Simon turned automatically to hand her up into the carriage. Mrs Coburn shook her head over the frivolous pair. They did not seem to her to be giving the business of escape the serious attention that it deserved.

On leaving the farmyard they must follow the lane that led to the Place for a good half mile. It was enough to sober them both. They drove in silence, alert and watchful, but though they saw one or two other travellers, no one paid them any particular heed. Presently they were able to relax a little. Harriet admired the new phaeton but expressed a fear that it was hardly the kind of vehicle in which one could escape notice. Simon rather meanly pointed out that with all eyes fixed on the phaeton no one would have any attention to spare for her. She chuckled, acknowledged a hit, and then wanted to know why he had brought so much baggage and which route they were to follow.

This time there was silence for a moment. Then he said gently, "It was the best I could devise. I have counted on your trusting yourself entirely to me."

One small hand rested impulsively on his

knee. "You know that I do. Have I not shown it?"

"And done me too much honour in so doing," he said soberly. Then went on swiftly, "To be blunt, disguised or not, the less you are seen in my society the better. We do not know when we may be glimpsed, recognised, remembered. The weather is fair and settled. I propose that we avoid inns and villages as much as possible. We can bivouac in barns, or copses if the night be clement. I have brought rugs and cushions and simple provisions—can purchase more as we need them. In this way we can travel unobtrusively if slowly. Carefully nursed my bays are good for thirty miles a day for we cannot risk changing horses. And as we must travel by quiet byways we may take up to six days in reaching our destination. However, so long as this dry weather holds you have nothing to fear but boredom."

She protested vigorously, saying with patent sincerity that she could think of no more idyllic method of passing the days of waiting. In fact, she was obviously of the mind that they need not trouble Miss Wilsher at all, but could just go gipsying along until her birthday arrived. Simon would dearly have liked to support this view, but he had already yielded far too readily to temptation. He should have escorted her to some rigidly proper hotel, hired a respectable abigail to wait on her and a sturdy groom and footman to protect her, and retired to keep watch and ward from a discreet distance so that the proprieties might be observed. He had seen this perfectly clearly and had refused to do it. Not to any one would he surrender the privilege of guarding her himself; of pretending, for a few stolen days, that she was his. She should never guess how dearly he loved her, but he would have—perhaps—a week, that he could cherish in memory for the rest of his days.

Fifteen

They spent a week in Arcady. Even the weather conspired to favour them. Each day dawned dew-crisp; the quiet lanes were a beguiling maze of sun and shade; the nights were still and cool. Harriet acquired a powdering of freckles on her nose, and the six days that Simon had allowed for the journey stretched into an inexcusable seven, while the horses were allowed to dawdle along in a most undisciplined fashion.

There was no word of lovemaking between them. Save for Simon's delicate care to spare his lady any small hardship, he treated her like the boy she pretended to be. They made a foolish joke about it, she calling herself Harry Dennis and boasting of various imaginary exploits, he devising ingenious punishment for her supposed escapades. Conversation might range from a deep discussion of moral principles to a lively argument as to the best way to fry eggs over a wood fire without acquiring the flavour of smoke. Often they lapsed into easy silence, each savouring present happiness, refusing to acknowledge the approaching shadow of desolation. As for Simon's care for her—well—she was his darling and his jewel and he would cherish her so, but his conduct seemed so natural, so simple that it oppressed her no more than a butterfly's touch. She was utterly at ease, without embarrassment or shyness. In the homely domestic pattern of making camp at some carefully chosen spot, of arranging their belongings in order while Simon tended the horses, of cooking—and arguing over—their evening meal, she bloomed into a new loveliness. Utterly content herself, she exhaled sweetness and warmth and sympathy as naturally as a flower pours out its scent. Simon adored her more with every passing minute. He never dreamed that all her sweetness stemmed from love of him, or that she thought herself too lowly to be his match in love.

During the week they came to a better understanding of each other's needs and natures than could ever have been possible in less intimate circumstances. Harriet talked quite openly of her life with the Cushings.

Simon had scarcely realised that such people existed. The conditions under which his beloved girl had lived and worked for five years quite appalled him. Yet gradually he came to see how the very harshness of the life had bred in her a philosophical elasticity of fibre, a toughness that guarded the tender heart. It won his deep respect. He understood that she had achieved for herself a freedom of spirit that many of her more fortunate contemporaries would never attain, and he wondered how he could ever have dismissed her tolerantly as a mere child. Once they talked of loneliness. Harriet described her feelings in her grandfather's luxurious home. Far worse, she contended, then with the Cushings. There she had been too busy to be lonely; and there was usually someone worse off than herself to pity or to comfort.

Simon spoke of his parents, and of how they had shared everything. His mother had even accompanied his father in some of his travels in the orient, enduring every discomfort and even occasional danger rather than be parted from him.

"That was the kind of marriage I dreamed of," he told her, lying stretched out beside the dying fire, his gaze on the dark arch of the heavens. "No room for loneliness there. My parents—oh—they did not always agree. I believe they argued quite fiercely at times. But because they truly loved each other it always ended in good humour and a little mild teasing, even though they still disagreed as strongly as ever."

He rolled over on one side, studying the slender boyish figure hunched in the fireglow, knees drawn up, arms clasped about them. The darkness was insidious, beguiling.

"Of late," he said abruptly, "I have been glad that I did not marry at twenty as I had hoped to do."

There was sympathy in the quiet darkness that made it easy to say things that one would not have ventured in broad daylight. Harriet too was tempted. She said tentatively, "Mrs Bedford told me about Lady Fiona. I saw her several times in London. She is very lovely."

"Very lovely indeed," confirmed Simon cheerfully. "But not the wife for me. I believe she and my brother go on very comfortably together, but perhaps they both enjoy a fashionable existence. He is certainly very proud of her. Now *I* should be a much more jealous spouse. I would want my wife for myself alone. No cicisbeos; no attendant court of masculine admirers. Parties and plays—yes—but I would be her escort. Worse! I would expect her to be interested in the running of Furzedown and the estate. The welfare of the tenants' families would be her particular concern, as it was my mother's." He broke off abruptly, with an awkward little laugh. "Just as well that I remained a bachelor, so exigeant a husband as I should have made!"

Harriet thought he sounded exactly the kind of husband for her—had she ever dared to raise her eyes so high. She sighed soundlessly and announced that she was sleepy and would go to bed.

So they came at last into Chippenham at dusk. The timing had been carefully planned, for tonight they must lie at a busy posting house. The busier the better, since Harry Dennis would go in at dusk and Miss Harriet Pendeniston would emerge next morning to make her curtsey to Miss Wilsher. The fewer people to witness this astonishing transformation, the better, and in the failing light not many would be sure whether they had seen a boy or a girl. And at first the plan worked well, most of the inn servants being occupied in serving late dinners or early suppers. Harriet was actually mounting the stairs to her chamber when disaster struck. As she reached a half-landing the door of a private parlour opened on to it, and a familiar voice said, "You need not come up with me, my dear. When I have the headache I am best left alone. A good night's sleep and I shall be perfectly well in the morning."

The door closed. The afflicted lady turned to mount the second flight, Harriet politely drawing back.

"Harriet!" exclaimed Lady Preston, shock and indignation mingling in her tones.

"Yes ma'am. Harry Dennis himself. Very much at your service," exclaimed Harriet with a hurried glance about her and performing quite a creditable bow.

Lady Preston, headache not withstanding, surveyed her from head to foot, making her blush for the first time since she had donned Mr Cushing's clothes.

"So I perceive," she said tartly. "And whither is Mr Dennis bound, if one may make so free? As an old acquaintance, of course."

There was an astringent touch in the voice that stung. Harriet said defensively, "Mr Dennis is so deeply indebted to Lady Preston that she may make what enquiries she wishes. But perhaps it would be better to do so in circumstances of greater privacy."

"I regret that I cannot invite you into the parlour," returned Lady Preston stiffly. "My niece would be a good deal shocked by such an encounter."

"Then will you honour me by sparing me a few moments in your bedchamber?" pleaded Harriet. "I promise you that no one has seen me closely, and that tomorrow Harry Dennis will have vanished. There will be no scandal, and indeed I can explain everything." Lady Preston looked far from convinced, but at least this odd encounter went far to cure a headache brought on largely by boredom.

She led the way to her room, but there was still a good deal of reserve in her manner.

"Your cousin has been in Bath seeking you," she said abruptly. "He thought you might have run to me. I do not know how you can say there will be no scandal, for he left here bound for Worthing. The story is bound to get about. I must say I was surprised that you should have behaved so, just when everything was going on so prosperously. You were not given to distempered freaks when you were in London."

But when Harriet had persuaded her to listen to the whole story, her sympathies veered sharply towards the narrator. Lord Halford had made no mention of the proposed marriage. He had told her ladyship that Harriet had run away because she objected to the rigid conventionality on which her grandfather insisted, and in doing so had caused her relatives to suffer grave anxiety for her well-being. In justice to herself and Simon, whose part in her escape she had not so far disclosed, Harriet told the blunt truth about the proposed marriage that was to be no marriage because of the bridegroom's preference for unnatural relations with his own sex. Lady Preston was deeply shocked, and when she learned how Harriet was to have been forced into this travesty of a marriage, she openly admitted that she did not blame her for running away.

"And to think that *I* persuaded you to visit your grandfather," she said remorsefully. "My dear, I wish I had never done so. For deeply as I sympathise with your feelings we cannot publish the story to the whole world, while the fact of your having run away is bound to leak out and every one will want to know the reason. But you haven't finished the story. How did you escape? Where did you run to, and where is Benworthy? If she is with you it may be possible to concoct some sort of a tale. Where have you been all this while?"

Well—she had always known that there would come a reckoning for that stolen week of heaven. She took a deep breath and embarked on further recital. The deepening dismay on Lady Preston's face as one damning fact was added to another, might have been comical if Harriet had not been so fond of her. For what had she done that was wrong? Reckless, perhaps, for she had known perfectly well that her own reputation was at stake, but certainly not wicked.

"And you have been all this time in Mr Warhurst's company? Quite unattended! And not even putting up at respectable inns but roving the countryside like a couple of gipsies. I never thought to hear of a young girl of sound principle lending herself to such a crazy start, let alone a great gentleman of Simon Warhurst's standing. I shall have something to say to that young man when next I see him."

She paused a while for reflection. Presently she went on slowly, "There is only one thing for it. We must get you married." Before Harriet could protest she added severely, "You would be very well served if I cast you off entirely, for your behaviour has been foolish and improper beyond belief, but I am willing to believe that you erred in innocence and since I persuaded you to go to your grandfather I feel myself in part responsible for the awkwardness of your situation. So I will see what can be contrived. You shall return to Bath with me. We shall be sadly cramped. My good-sister's house is not large. And Bath is quiet just now. There are still one or two eligible gentlemen who reside there permanently, so I do not wholly despair of making up a respectable match for you. Benworthy must bring your clothes and"—she broke off as Harriet shook her head vigorously. "Now what objection can you have to *that*, pray?"

"It would be to betray my whereabouts to my grandfather, and he has legal rights over me until I come of age, which is not for another week."

"Oh, very well. We must make shift without Benworthy. I daresay there wouldn't have been room for her anyway," snapped Lady Preston irritably. "What a tiresome chit you are! What can your grandfather do in a week?

If I were in his position I would wash my hands of you and look elsewhere for a bride for that horrid young man."

But Harriet, who had experienced something of the colonel's ruthless determination, could not be reassured. "It will be much safer for me to stay hid with Miss Wilsher. And indeed I would not put you to so much trouble, for I have made up my mind to it that I shall not marry. In any case, how could I honourably accept an offer when you yourself have said that the scandal is bound to leak out? Think of the poor gentleman's feelings."

Lady Preston grudgingly admitted that there was something in this argument. "But it is nonsense to say that you have decided not to marry. I shall think of some way out of the tangle," she promised determinedly. "Now you may kiss me goodnight. Go to bed—and don't fall into any more scrapes." So that Harriet was able to count herself forgiven and retire to her room with an easier mind.

Sixteen

A note delivered by a chambermaid informed her that she was to breakfast with her two protectors in Lady Preston's parlour, and urged to try to present a respectable appearance. It promised to be a lively meal, she thought, with a good deal of brisk skirmishing about her plans and prospects. It was difficult to do much about her appearance with only one well-worn dress and shabby shoes, but she dressed her hair very neatly in one of her more feminine styles, and went down to the private parlour wearing her most demure expression.

Lady Preston's militant bearing and a certain tension in the atmosphere informed her that sparks had been flying, but her ladyship greeted her with a smile and Simon rose to pull out her chair and enquire her choice among the various dishes with his customary ease. The niece to whom Lady Preston had referred on the previous evening was not present. Presumably she had been told to take breakfast in her own room. The decks had been cleared for action.

While she ate she was informed that her ladyship had kindly charged herself with the task of buying her a new dress and cloak and one or two other indispensable articles so that she could enter upon her stay with Miss Wilsher fittingly equipped.

It was the last straw. She hesitated only briefly, sighed sharply, and decided to speak her mind. Ever since Simon had pulled her out of the river she had been the recipient of charity in one form of another. The time had come to call a halt.

"It is quite unnecessary," she said. "If you will lend me a needle and thread and a pair of scissors, this dress can be made perfectly presentable and I can easily mend the rent in my cloak. In a week's time—less—I shall be starting a new life, seeking a new post. I know, better than either of you, how I should be dressed for that new life, and this dress is perfectly suitable. It is a little too fine, perhaps, but it is just such a dress as might have been bestowed upon me by an indulgent mistress when she had tired of it, and it will serve very well. I am sure that Miss Wilsher will perfectly understand my position, and since I do not propose to go out of doors while I am staying with her, she will not be embarrassed by my shabbiness."

There was a brief stunned silence. Where Harriet was concerned, both Simon and Lady Preston were accustomed to making the decisions. It was a shock to discover that the days of such guardianship were over. Lady Preston spread her hands in a gesture of resignation. Simon was made of sterner stuff.

He smiled at her ladyship and said pleasantly, "If you will proceed precisely as we planned, I will undertake to bring Harriet to a better frame of mind."

Lady Preston was only too thankful to do so. "Then I shall set out at once," she announced cheerfully, "and I shall take my niece with me. You may use my parlour for your scolding, and I wish you joy of it."

For a long moment Simon studied the beloved little face; saw the new maturity, the quiet determination, and knew it would not be easy. This was no child to be cleverly cajoled, but a woman who had chosen her path and would hold to it. He needed something stronger than sensible arguments.

He said slowly, "A week ago you came to me in distress and begged my help. You placed yourself unreservedly in my hands, asking me to devise a plan to save you from your enemies. So far as I was able, I have done what you asked. Perhaps you will tell me where I have erred to cause you to withdraw your confidence."

The sudden and completely unexpected attack penetrated to the heart. She forgot all about the stubborn resistance that she had meant to oppose to all persuasions. She flushed scarlet, stammering in her earnestness as she exclaimed, "Why, n-nothing. You have been everything that is kind and ch-chivalrous."

"Then why are you so determined to shake off my assistance and ignore my advice? You might just as well have slapped my face."

It was too much. Try as she might her eyes glistened with tears scarce held back, and her voice was husky with them as she said humbly, "I will do as you wish, Sir. Indeed I cannot endure your displeasure." And then, on a sob hurriedly gulped back, "You must believe that. Please! Especially after this last wonderful week. You must know that I would do anything to serve you—to bring you happiness."

There was a deep silence. Then Simon's voice, queerly strained, said slowly, "Anything?"

Her face brightened a little, though two tears slid down her cheeks. "Yes. Anything. I can imagine no greater joy than to serve you and to bring you contentment."

The words were deliberately chosen, long rehearsed. Her ambitions were lowly. But when other gentlemen had admired her she had sometimes dreamed that Mr Warhurst might yet succumb to a similar weakness and would perhaps take her for his mistress. If that day ever came, she would yield to him gladly, proudly. Was she not his by right? But for him she must have died. If thoughts of personal bliss tended to modify the magnitude of the sacrifice, she dismissed them as sinful. Poor Harriet was more naive than she dreamed. Now she awaited his decision, half-eager, half-frightened.

He said quietly, "Are you willing so far to honour me as to consent to be my wife?"

The suggestion shocked her into silence. Even in her most extravagant dreams she had never imagined this. Before she could recover from her stunned amaze he went on, "I am too old for you, I know. A rustic oaf, dull and set in my ways, but I promise that I will do all that a man may to make up to you for the sacrifice of your youth and beauty."

Somehow she found her voice. "No sacrifice," she said in a husky little whisper. "If you really mean it, then to stay with you always, to belong to you, would be such happiness as I never dreamed to win."

He gazed at her disbelievingly for a moment. Her face was glowing into tremulous new-born happiness. She put out a tentative hand towards him and was drawn gently into his arms.

"You are quite sure?" she whispered. "I am no match for you, I know, though no one could love you more dearly. Only I had thought—you are nobly born and a great gentleman—you n-need not marry me, you know."

There was nothing gentle about the grasp on her hand now. It hardened to steely strength as his arms tightened about her.

"Never let me hear such nonsense on your lips again," he said harshly, and crushed the soft mouth with his lest she should venture to disobey.

She had loved him so long and so hopelessly. A sweet melting warmth suffused her body. She was pliant and willing in his arms, and if she was all untaught in the ways of love she was an eager pupil. Simon had been long starved of such delights. He put her from him a little unsteadily. "We can be married on your birthday," he planned swiftly. "A special licence—that's the thing."

"No marriage portion," reminded Harriet with a glimmer of mischief. "Grandfather will certainly disinherit me once and for all."

"And a good thing too. It took all my courage to ask you to marry a man ten years older than yourself. Had you been an heiress as well, I doubt I could never have ventured it."

"Then grandfather has done me a true kindness at last," pointed out Harriet, and slipped her hand confidingly into his.

Let COVENTRY Give You
A Little Old-Fashioned Romance

	Title	No.	Price
☐	HOTSPUR & TAFFETA by Claudette Williams	50186	$1.9
☐	A SANDITON QUADRILLE by Rebecca Baldwin	50187	$1.9
☐	THREE LOVES by Sylvia Thorpe	50188	$1.9
☐	CATHERINE by Audrey Blanshard	50189	$1.9
☐	JESSABELLE by Maggie MacKeever	50190	$1.9
☐	THE BARTERED BRIDEGROOM by Georgina Grey	50191	$1.9

Buy them at your local bookstore or use this handy coupon for ordering.

COLUMBIA BOOK SERVICE
32275 Mally Road, P.O. Box FB, Madison Heights, MI 48071

Please send me the books I have checked above. Orders for less than 5 boo must include 75¢ for the first book and 25¢ for each additional book to cov postage and handling. Orders for 5 books or more postage is FREE. Send che or money order only.

Cost $________ Name ________________________

Sales tax*________ Address ________________________

Postage ________ City ________________________

Total $________ State ________________ Zip ________

The government requires us to collect sales tax in all states except AK, D MT, NH and OR.

This offer expires 1 March 82 **817**

CURRENT CREST BESTSELLERS

Title	No.	Price
] THE NINJA *by Eric Van Lustbader*	24367	$3.50
] SHOCKTRAUMA *by Jon Franklin & Alan Doelp*	24387	$2.95
] KANE & ABEL *Jeffrey Archer*	24376	$3.75
] PRIVATE SECTOR *Jeff Millar*	24368	$2.95
] DONAHUE *Phil Donahue & Co.*	24358	$2.95
] DOMINO *Phyllis A. Whitney*	24350	$2.75
] TO CATCH A KING *Harry Patterson*	24323	$2.95
] AUNT ERMA'S COPE BOOK *Erma Bombeck*	24334	$2.75
] THE GLOW *Brooks Stanwood*	24333	$2.75
] RESTORING THE AMERICAN DREAM *Robert J. Ringer*	24314	$2.95
] THE LAST ENCHANTMENT *Mary Stewart*	24207	$2.95
] CENTENNIAL *James A. Michener*	23494	$2.95
] THE COUP *John Updike*	24259	$2.95
] THURSDAY THE RABBI WALKED OUT *Harry Kemelman*	24070	$2.25
] IN MY FATHER'S COURT *Isaac Bashevis Singer*	24074	$2.50
] A WALK ACROSS AMERICA *Peter Jenkins*	24277	$2.75
] WANDERINGS *Chaim Potok*	24270	$3.95

uy them at your local bookstore or use this handy coupon for ordering.

OLUMBIA BOOK SERVICE
2275 Mally Road, P.O. Box FB, Madison Heights, MI 48071

lease send me the books I have checked above. Orders for less than 5 books
ıust include 75¢ for the first book and 25¢ for each additional book to cover
ostage and handling. Orders for 5 books or more postage is FREE. Send check
r money order only.

Cost $________ Name ____________________

Sales tax*________ Address ____________________

Postage ________ City ____________________

Total $________ State ____________ Zip ________

The government requires us to collect sales tax in all states except AK, DE, MT, NH and OR.

his offer expires 1 March 82 **8177**

CURRENT BESTSELLERS from POPULAR LIBRARY

☐ INNOCENT BLOOD by P. D. James 04630 $3.5
☐ FALLING IN PLACE by Ann Beattie 04650 $2.9
☐ THE FATHER OF FIRES by Kenneth M. Cameron 04640 $2.9
☐ WESTERN WIND by Oliver B. Patton 04634 $2.9
☐ HAWKS by Joseph Amiel 04620 $2.9
☐ LOVE IS JUST A WORD by Johannes Mario Simmel 04622 $2.9
☐ THE SENDAI by William Woolfolk 04628 $2.7
☐ NIGHT WATCH by Jack Olsen 04609 $2.7
☐ THE GREAT SHARK HUNT by Hunter S. Thompson 04596 $3.5
☐ THE WOTAN WARHEAD by James Follett 04629 $2.5
☐ TO THE HONOR OF THE FLEET by Robert H. Pilpel 04576 $2.9

Buy them at your local bookstore or use this handy coupon for ordering.

COLUMBIA BOOK SERVICE
32275 Mally Road, P.O. Box FB, Madison Heights, MI 48071

Please send me the books I have checked above. Orders for less than 5 boo must include 75¢ for the first book and 25¢ for each additional book to cov postage and handling. Orders for 5 books or more postage is FREE. Send che or money order only.

Cost $______ Name ______

Sales tax*______ Address ______

Postage ______ City ______

Total $______ State ______ Zip ______

**The government requires us to collect sales tax in all states except AK, D MT, NH and OR.*

This offer expires 1 March 82 **81**